I0522577

BOOTS & BUCKLES

UGLY STICK SALOON SERIES BOOK #9

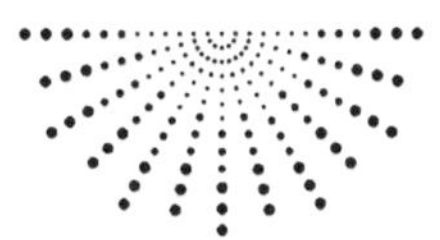

MYLA JACKSON

TWISTED PAGE INC

BOOTS & BUCKLES

UGLY STICK SALOON SERIES BOOK #9

New York Times & *USA Today*
Bestselling Author

ELLE JAMES

writing as

MYLA JACKSON

Copyright © 2017 by Myla Jackson

Copyright © 2014 previously published by Samhain Publishing

All rights reserved.

No part of this book may be reproduced in any form or by any electronic or mechanical means, including information storage and retrieval systems, without written permission from the author, except for the use of brief quotations in a book review.

EBOOK ISBN: 978-1-62695-100-6

PRINT ISBN: 978-1-62695-101-3

This book is dedicated to strong, independent women who want to make a better life for themselves and find someone to share it without taking away their own identity.

AUTHOR'S NOTE

Enjoy other Ugly Stick Saloon books by Myla Jackson
Ugly Stick Saloon Series
Boots & Chaps (#1)
Boots & Sex Ed (#2)
Boots & Leather (#3)
Boots & Promises (#4)
Boots & Bareback (#5)
Boots & Dirty Tricks (#6)
Boots & Lace (#7)
Boots & Roses (#8)
Boots & Buckles (#9)
Boots & the Wishes (#10)
Boots & Twisters (#11)
Boots & the Bachelor (#12)
Boots & The Rogue (#13)
Boots & The Heartbreaker (#14)
Boots & Wings (#15)

Visit Mylajackson.com for more information
Visit her alter ego Elle James at ellejames.com
Join Elle James and Myla Jackson's Newsletter at
http://ellejames.com/ElleContact.htm

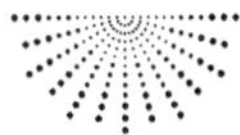

Grant saw her as soon as he stepped through the door. Just like it had been when he'd seen her for the first time, he'd been drawn to Mona's smile and the way she moved with a sexy flare she wasn't even aware of.

The three years since he'd last been to Temptation hadn't changed her much. Perhaps she was a little thinner, but she was just as beautiful as the day they'd met at the Ugly Stick Saloon during Tri-County Rodeo week. He and his then-partner, Dalton Faulkner, had been there for the rodeo. She'd been helping out at the Ugly Stick, waiting tables and serving drinks to rowdy cowboys fresh off the adrenaline rush of roping steers, riding bulls or broncs.

He chose the table in the back of the saloon because it *wasn't* one that Mona was servicing. His waitress, Kendall, was a sweet young thing he didn't recognize from his last visit to the saloon. She wore a diamond engagement ring on her finger and didn't take any lip or advances from the horny men raising hell after a tough day in the saddle.

"This place is great." His new team roping partner, Sam Whitefeather, tipped his long neck and swallowed the last of the beer in one gulp, slapped the bottle on the table and pushed to his feet. "You stickin' around for a while?"

"Yeah, why?"

"Could you order me another? I'm gonna hit the latrine." Sam reached for his wallet.

Grant held up his hand. "I'll get this round. Go."

He'd skipped the last two years' rodeos here because he couldn't bring himself to face Mona. The first year, because his life had been a mess, his career as a team roper at an end when he and Dalton had parted ways, and his bronc riding on the verge of collapse.

If not for Sam, he'd have found some bottle to crawl into and given up on everything. It took him the next couple years of total focus and concentration to regain his credibility and top rating in the competitions. Only then had he felt like he could return and see if there was anything left to salvage between him and Mona.

The woman foremost on his mind walked by carrying a tray of beer mugs and long necks, and his heart flipped over, reminding Grant of everything he'd lost and all the mistakes he'd made. He tipped his hat lower over his forehead, not ready to let her see him. Not sure what he expected to get out of coming back to Temptation. Would she ever forgive him for making promises he didn't keep?

MONA PLUNKED her tray of empty beer bottles and mugs on the bar and gave Libby, the bartender, her order for the next round to be delivered.

Audrey Anderson, the owner of the Ugly Stick Saloon, slipped in beside her, carrying her own tray of empties. "Mona, thanks so much for helping out during rodeo week."

"No, Audrey. I should be thanking you. I don't know what I would have done without you."

"You really don't think Old Man Spillman will extend the lease on your salon?"

"I've already asked. I have a thirty-day option to buy and Spillman is ready to sell. If I don't agree to buy it in that thirty days, the old coot is going to take the first reasonable offer."

"How much are you short?"

"I have to come up with at least another grand to add to my meager savings before the bank will even consider loaning me the money to buy the building."

"I can spot you the money."

Mona shook her head. "I can't let you do that. You've already done so much for me and half the people in town. If I can't find a way to earn the money, I don't deserve to buy the salon."

"I could use you all week, if that will help."

"I'm all yours. I can come in after six every evening when I close the Shear Safari."

"Make it at least by nine and stay until midnight. That's when things are craziest and the men tip better."

Audrey emptied her tray and slid behind the counter to help Libby fill her next round of orders.

Libby loaded Mona's tray and nodded. "You're good to go."

Mona lifted the heavy tray, balancing it carefully.

"Oh, and Mona," Audrey called out, "if you're interested in making more in a single night, I might have some exotic dancing gigs coming up. The rodeo winners usually hire some of the girls to dance at their parties."

Mona bit her lip. She'd danced for Audrey before, but now that she had her own business as a hair stylist, she'd decided the dancing jobs might offend potential customers. But with her salon at risk of closing, a girl had to take risks she normally wouldn't. "Let me know, and I'll think about it."

Audrey nodded. "I will. And no worries if you decide not to do it."

"Thanks." Mona turned and wove her way through the rowdy cowboys, some still wearing jeans and boots covered in rodeo dust. Others had taken the extra time to come showered, polished and dressed in their pearl-buttoned snap shirts, sporting their trophy belt buckles won that day or on the circuit.

Mona had her ass pinched more times than she could count. After a three-year sabbatical on dating, she'd about convinced herself she should try it again. Or rather Bunny Leigh's experience with the date she'd bid on at the Annual Cowboy Auction had convinced Mona it was time to get over the cowboy she'd foolishly given her heart to, and move on.

But now wasn't good. Not during the circus of Tri-County Rodeo week. She'd learned her lesson three years ago not to believe a rodeo cowboy any farther than she could throw him. She'd made the mistake of falling in love with a very handsome team roper. Like all the cry-in-your-beer songs played, he'd broken her heart.

Mona served the cowboys with a polite smile, enough to get a good tip, but not enough to encourage them to ask her out. She picked up the empty bottles from a table, setting them onto her empty tray.

"Have you seen the news?" one of the cowboys said to the other.

With the band playing loud enough to make the men shout to be heard, Mona couldn't help overhearing their conversation.

"Nah, haven't been near a television for two days. What's up?"

"Raleigh's competin' on broncs, and he and the Indian are paired up for team ropin'."

"Whatever happened between him and his team ropin' partner Faulkner? Not that I'm sorry they busted up. Gives the rest of us a fighting chance to win."

"Faulkner is riding bulls these days. He's here too. Should be up on the bulls tomorrow."

Mona's hand shook. The bottle she'd just grabbed slipped from her fingers and bounced off the table.

The cowboy sitting in the seat beside her grabbed the bottle before it hit the floor and grinned up at her. "Careful there, pretty thing." He set the bottle on her tray and winked. "Don't suppose you'd dance with this old cowboy, wouldja?"

Her heart pounding against her ribs and her knees wobbling, Mona could only shake her head before she turned and hurried away.

She didn't know how she'd gotten back to the bar with all the bottles and mugs intact. Tossing the empties in the trash, she slid her tray across the bar and leaned against the counter, afraid her knees would buckle and she'd fall flat on her face.

"Hey, sweetie, you look as if you've seen a ghost." Bunny Leigh sat in the barstool beside her and frowned. "What's wrong?"

"Oh, Bunny, I just heard *they're* gonna be here."

"Who?" Bunny glanced around the saloon. "Where?"

Mona turned her back to the bar and stared around the shadowy interior of the saloon, searching and thankfully not finding them. "Grant Raleigh and Dalton Faulkner. They're competing in the rodeo!"

"Grant and Dalton?" Bunny's brows rose. "As in the love-'em-and-cheat-'em cowboys who broke your heart three years ago?"

Letting out a long slow breath, Mona fought to steady her racing pulse. "They're the ones." Well, at least one of them broke her heart. Grant.

Bunny spun on her stool and studied the crowd of cowboys, a fierce glare pressing her brows together. "Where are they? I want to give them a piece of my mind."

She looked so much like a bull terrier guarding her

bone that Mona laughed. "I doubt they'll show up around here. They're big shots now. Grant's won just about every bronc riding competition on the circuit and all the western wear outfitters are clamoring for him to represent them. And Dalton's been the reigning bull rider with his own line of boots. I doubt he'll have time to stop by for a beer."

"That and Grant's wife probably has some pull in keeping him home at night." Bunny snorted. "Would have been nice if he'd let you know he was engaged before he and Dalton started dating you."

"I should have known better than to date rodeo cowboys." Mona's lips twisted. "My mamma warned me about them a long time ago. Guess I had to learn for myself."

Audrey returned to the bar, followed by Charli Sutton. Both women set their empty trays behind the bar.

"The band is on break. It's that time, ladies," Audrey called out.

Libby and Audrey cleared the bar quickly and turned on the music for the night's performance. Audrey, Charli, Lacey, Kendall and Libby climbed up on the bar.

Audrey waved to Mona. "Come on, you know the routine."

Mona shook her head.

Bunny shoved her forward. "Get up there and show them that you don't care about them anymore. You've moved on. There are dozens of cowboys in this room that would give their left nut to be with you."

"Yeah, and then they'll move on to the next rodeo, the next buckle bunny—no offense."

"None taken." Bunny grinned. "Get up there and have some fun."

Mona hesitated a second longer, glancing around the saloon, half-hoping she would see Dalton and Grant at the same time as she prayed they'd stay clear of the Ugly Stick throughout the rodeo.

As the music started, Mona threw her doubts to the Texas wind, hopped up on the bar and danced to the strains of "Save a Horse, Ride a Cowboy".

To hell with falling for heartbreakers. Tonight she'd break a few of her own.

SAM STEPPED out of the latrine to the sound of raucous shouting and loud bump-and-grind music. All the cowboys were turned toward the bar where the waitresses danced in unison in short-shorts, tight tank tops, cowboy hats and cowboy boots.

"Nice." Sam stood back several deep in the crowd, grinning. He'd never been to this part of Texas and the Ugly Stick Saloon had proven to be one of the friendliest bars he'd ever been inside. Not all bars welcomed Native Americans, though he preferred to be referred to as a Lakotan, but he'd felt right at home among the cowboys here.

And the pretty brunette waitress on the end seemed to smile right at him. What would it take to get that one to dance with him?

The woman in the middle wearing bright red, metal-studded cowboy boots, called out, "Catch a hat and dance with one of the lovely ladies of the Ugly Stick." The song ended, the ladies all yelled, "Yee-haw!" and flung their hats into the crowd.

Standing six feet five inches, Sam had no trouble snatching the one thrown by the brunette on the end and considered it a sign from *Wakatanka*, the Great Spirit, that he was meant to meet this woman and dance with her.

The cowboys parted to allow him to pluck the waitress off the bar and set her on her feet.

"Hello, I'm Mona Daley." She stuck out her hand.

"Sam Whitefeather." He plunked her hat on her head, took her hand and shook it. Someone bumped her from behind and she fell against his chest. Sam chuckled and held her steady until she got her feet under her and straightened her hat. He liked the way she smelled of honeysuckle and citrus.

The band struck up a slow song and the cowboys who'd caught the hats led the waitresses onto the dance floor. Sam followed, Mona's hand held snuggly in his.

She glanced up at him with pretty brown eyes. "Do you two-step?"

In answer, he lifted her hand, rested his other hand on the small of her back and swept her onto the dance floor, thanking his sister for insisting he help her learn how to dance. With their father working two jobs to make ends meet and feed them as well as the horses, Sam filled the gap his mother's early demise had created. Now that Gemma was out of high school and halfway through college at University of North Dakota,

Sam could have a little fun and loosen up on his sense of responsibility for his kid sister.

Ah hell, who was he trying to kid? Gemma was part of the reason he'd gotten into rodeoing. It helped pay her way through school and kept his father out of debt. And none of it would have been possible if Grant hadn't collapsed in a drunken stupor outside a bar in Minot, North Dakota, during rodeo week.

He owed his current way of life to Grant, but the feeling was mutual. If Sam hadn't picked him up out of the gravel, shoved him into his truck and taken him to the Whitefeather Ranch, Grant might have died of exposure that night in the parking lot. And if not exposure, he might have crawled back into the bottle he'd been wallowing in and lost everything.

Now, Sam and Grant were on top of the rodeo world, winning big cash prizes and sponsorship deals at every rodeo. Grant pushed them as if he had an evil spirit on his tail he couldn't shake.

Sam suspected it had something to do with his ex-wife and his ex-partner. Only Grant had never filled him in on those parts of his past and Sam hadn't pushed.

With the pretty Mona in his arms, he didn't want to look back, only forward to this dance and maybe more.

"Are you with the rodeo?" Mona asked with a smile.

"I am."

Her smile faded a bit then reappeared. "That's nice. What events do you participate in?"

"Team roping and bull ridin'." He inhaled her scent

again, liking the way it wafted around him as they moved in a wide circle around the dance floor.

"You must meet a lot of people on the circuit," she commented, her gaze leaving his, her smile appearing more strained.

"I do. But none as pretty as you." His hand tightened around hers.

"Uh-huh. I'll bet you say that to all the girls you dance with." This time her smile was gone and she gazed directly into his eyes.

"No, just the ones who deserve it." He spun her away from him and back into his arms, holding her closer, his hips moving against hers. "Do you have a problem with rodeo cowboys?"

"Not anymore." She tossed her hair back over her shoulder. "You know, once burned, don't stand so close to the fire."

"And a rodeo cowboy burned you?" His fingers squeezed hers.

"Something like that." Her gaze went past him, as if looking into her memories.

He leaned close and whispered into her ear, "I'm not here to burn you, Mona. I only want to dance with you."

She blinked up at him, her eyes shimmering with unshed tears. "Then shut up and dance."

Sam's chest tightened at the sadness he witnessed in her valiant attempt to pretend to be happy and carefree. This woman who fit so well against his body had been hurt badly by someone. The protector in him wanted to find that someone and break every bone in his body.

As the music came to a halt, Sam didn't want to let go. "One more dance?"

She shook her head. "Sorry, I have to get back to the tables. Those men can get pretty thirsty."

He held on to her hand as she spun away, dragging her back to his side. "Where can I find you during the day? I'd like to see you again."

"Sorry, I don't go out with rodeo cowboys." When she tried to jerk her hand free, he pulled her against his chest and kissed her lips.

GRANT'S HEART squeezed in his chest as Mona danced on the bar with the other women of the Ugly Stick Saloon and when she'd tossed her hat, he wanted to be the one to catch it, but he held back. The timing wasn't right. He wanted to get her alone and talk to her in private. See how she was, if she still had any feelings for him. If not, he knew he had to move on. This wouldn't be the place where he'd set down roots and retire. Not if he couldn't have Mona at his side.

When his partner had caught her hat and escorted her to the dance floor, Grant's gut knotted. Sam was as close as a friend could be. He's saved his sorry ass from self-destruction. And now he was dancing with the only woman Grant had ever loved.

When the music came to a halt, Grant rose to his feet, with some half-baked thought of going to Mona and demanding she not fall in love with his partner on the tip of his tongue.

Then Sam bent and kissed Mona. On her lips.

The air sucked out of Grant's lungs in a whoosh and he collapsed back in his chair.

Mona's eyes rounded and she reached up and slapped Sam in the face so hard the clap could be heard over the rumble of music and conversation of the rodeo cowboys. All eyes turned toward the pair on the dance floor. Sam's jaw tightened momentarily, then he smiled and dipped his head. "My apologies, ma'am."

The room erupted into loud raucous laughter and cowboys slapped Sam's back on his way back to the table he shared with Grant.

As Sam took his seat, he rubbed his cheek. "I deserved that."

Grant grunted, afraid if he said anything, he'd reveal more than he wanted. Hopefully, the slap on the face would discourage his partner from wanting to see Mona again.

As Sam rubbed the bright red handprint on his cheek, his face split in a grin. "That lady's got spunk. I'm gonna ask her out."

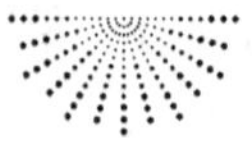

CHAPTER TWO

Audrey pulled Mona aside as soon as she returned to the bar. "Did that cowboy make a pass at you? Do you want me to have Jackson take him out back and teach him some manners?"

Mona laughed and pressed her stinging hand to her cheek. "No, no. That won't be necessary. I overreacted. He was just thanking me for the dance."

"Still, I don't like customers taking liberties with my girls." Audrey's eyes narrowed. "I think I'll have a word with him myself."

Mona grabbed her arm. "No, really. I'm fine and he won't do it again. It was just a knee-jerk reaction on my part. These rodeos bring back so many memories."

Audrey pulled her into her arms and hugged her. "I know, sweetie. I shouldn't have asked you to help out. I know how hard it is."

Bunny joined the hug, wrapping her arms around

them. "Mona, honey, did that big ol' hunk of a cowboy kiss you?"

Mona rolled her eyes. "As if everyone in the saloon didn't witness that kiss and my reaction. Yes, he did."

"And?" Bunny stood back, her brows raised. "How'd it feel?"

Mona's immediate response should have been, *Terrible*. But she chewed on her lip and a smile broke loose. "Not bad."

"See? You're ready to get back out there. To hell with Grant and Dalton. You're young, beautiful and deserve to find a little love." Bunny pounded her back.

Mona winced at the force of Bunny's exuberance.

Audrey's brows twisted. "Bunny's right. It's been three years. You really should give yourself a second chance. Not all cowboys are losers."

"Yeah, but Sam is a rodeo cowboy. You know the routine…a girl in every town. I don't want that. I'll find a man here in Temptation. One who isn't going to up and leave me for the next town, the next woman." She sighed. "Although Sam's arms were really strong and he was so tall I couldn't see over his shoulders."

"So what's it going to hurt to see a guy like that? It's not like you're going to marry him," Bunny noted. "You could practice your moves on him while you're looking for a man to settle down with."

Mona looked at her friend as if she'd had one too many. "That sounds so calculating. I couldn't do that to him."

"Why not? Rodeo cowboys would do it to you."

Mona tapped a finger to her chin. "Yeah, they would, wouldn't they?"

"Now you're thinking." Bunny clapped her hands. "Have a little fun. If you tell them upfront you're not looking for commitment, it's not calculating. You're pretty, single, over twenty-one and, honey, you're not gettin' any younger."

"Hey." Mona backhanded Bunny in the belly. "You could have left off that last comment. I'm not long in the tooth."

Audrey shook her head. "Flirt, go out with the guy, do whatever you're going to do later. Right now, I've got thirsty customers ready to spend their money on drinks and tips. Get back to work." She grinned as she shoved a tray in Mona's hands.

Mona dove back into working her tables, keeping an eye out for the tall, dark and handsome cowboy who'd dared to kiss her. Not that he'd want anything to do with her now, after she'd slapped his face in front of God and everyone.

The Ugly Stick was so packed, she didn't see him again. But she knew the moment Dalton Faulkner stepped through the entrance. After three long years, he still made her heart flutter, a little. Just as tall as he'd been and still as devastatingly handsome with his sandy blond hair and startling blue eyes. She'd seen him since his and Grant's break up as a team, plastered on billboards in cowboy boot ads along the highways and in commercials.

Every woman in the place turned to stare as he

waded through the crowd, shaking hands and smiling like a prince working a crowd of his subjects.

Too bad it was all an act. The man was out for only one thing. Himself. And whatever woman would fall into his bed at the crook of his finger. Too bad Mona hadn't seen his true nature sooner. She halfway expected it from him then, but not from Grant. He'd seemed more stable and sincere.

"Did you see?" Bunny slipped up beside Mona as she removed the empty bottles and mugs from her tray and gave Libby her order.

"I did." Mona turned to watch as a cowboy got up to offer Dalton his chair in a saloon that had become standing-room only. "Do you think they hope his magic will rub off on them?"

"Yeah, when you're on a roll in the rodeo business, you're like gods. Too bad it went to Dalton's head." Bunny turned her friend around. "You're over him, aren't you?"

"Oh, yeah. I'm completely over him." She said it like she meant it, but that flutter of butterflies in her belly made her wonder if she truly was. Maybe she should test the waters and see if they had really cooled.

"He's sitting at one of your tables, you want me to take the tray?" Bunny offered. She'd worked the Ugly Stick before when she'd needed money to tide her over during a cash flow crunch at her florist business.

"No, thank you. I need to prove to myself I'm well and truly over him. No time like the present." Armed with the feel of a handsome cowboy's kiss still tingling on her lips, she marched over to the table where Dalton sat and settled the mugs and bottles in front of the cowboys who'd ordered them. "Can I get you anything?"

"Mona, baby!" Dalton grabbed her around the middle and dragged her into his lap. "I missed you so much. Give me a kiss."

When he would have pressed his lips to hers, she shoved the flat side of her tray up into his face. "I'm sorry, kisses and groping will cost you extra," she said in what she hoped was a flippant tone when she really wanted to crash the tray over his head. The man hadn't changed.

The men around the table laughed heartily.

Dalton's face reddened, but he laughed, though it sounded forced. "Just the way I like 'em. Sassy!" He slapped her thigh.

He was a complete, arrogant bastard and what she'd ever seen in him was beyond her comprehension at that moment. Had she been blind? Or too besotted that someone that popular in the media's eye would have anything to do with the girl from a small town in Texas?

Mona shoved Dalton's hands away from her and hopped out of his lap. "Do you want a drink? If not, I have work to do."

He gave his order and Mona escaped. When she made it back to the bar, Bunny was there, eyes wide. "I thought you were going to hit him with your tray."

"I almost did." Mona glanced back at Dalton then smiled at Bunny. "It's official."

"What?"

"I'm over him."

Bunny clapped her hands and hugged her. "Good,

then you can go after that other cowboy with an open heart and mind."

Mona frowned. "I have yet to see Grant." And if truth be told, he was the one Mona was more concerned about seeing. Looking back, it was Grant's tenderness and caring that had brought her close to the team roping pair. In the end, he'd been no different than Dalton, running out on her without looking back. It had been Grant who'd made all the promises then broken them. In which case, it made him an even bigger heel than Dalton. Not that it mattered. Three years was a long time. Hell, he probably wouldn't even recognize her.

"Grant, Schmant. You're ready. If he has the gall to show up here, you can tell him exactly what you think of him and be free and clear of any lingering heartache." Bunny looked around the room. "Have you seen him?"

"No. As far as that goes, I haven't even seen the cowboy since our little dance."

Bunny frowned and glanced around the saloon. "Wonder where he got off to?"

"Doesn't matter. There are a hundred guys in the room. Why should I worry about one or two?"

"That's my Mona. She's back in the saddle!" Bunny grabbed her tray from her hand and slammed it on the bar. "Come on, I want to dance, but I don't want to do it alone."

"Yeah, really, where are Cory and Jack?"

"Cory had a big test to study for his medical school in Dallas and won't be home all week. Jack is on duty tonight since it's rodeo week. I'm partnerless."

"I'm sure any one of these cowboys would love to dance with you." Mona let Bunny drag her toward the dance floor.

"Yeah, but not all of them know the steps to this line dance, and you do." She jumped into the lines of cowboys and cowgirls kicking up their feet to a lively country song, all in sync with the dance steps. In time with the music, they all yelled, "Hell, yeah!"

Mona laughed and clapped her hands when she was supposed to and spun and did the grapevine. She'd let her life become too mundane, too predictable, it was time she had a little more fun.

As she danced with Bunny, she just happened to glance toward the far corner of the bar, right into Grant Raleigh's ice blue eyes.

"Do you think she'll give me her number after slapping my face?" Sam asked, with his back to the dance floor.

Grant's radar had picked up on Mona as soon as she stepped onto the dance floor with a woman Grant recognized but couldn't put a name to. As the line dance progressed, Mona got into the moves, her hips swinging, her smile bright.

Grant's jeans tightened. He remembered how Mona felt beneath him, her hips in his hands as he thrust into her while she sucked on Dalton's cock. That she'd been willing to go to bed with the two of them made him hot then and even hotter as he watched her dancing.

When her gaze met his, Grant froze, his breath caught in his throat. She recognized him immediately.

She stopped in mid-step, her gaze going from surprise to shock. The rest of the dancers bumped into her, she tripped on her own boots and tried to catch herself, taking down half the line like a row of dominoes.

Grant leaped from his seat.

"What the hell?" Sam exclaimed and jumped up after him.

Pushing his way through the crowd, Grant emerged onto the dance floor.

Mona lay in a tangled heap of boots, legs and laughing people. She struggled to get her feet back under her, cringing as someone stepped on her leg.

Grant held out his hand. "Take my hand."

She looked up at him, her face blanching, and hesitated.

Sam arrived at his side and lunged in, lifting her to her feet. "Mona, are you okay?" He pulled her into his arms and brushed the hair out of her eyes.

Another woman grabbed Grant's hand and pulled herself to her feet, pretending to trip so that she could wrap her arms around his neck. She kissed his cheek. "Thanks. I don't know what happened." She laughed. "All the sudden I was in a dog pile on the floor."

Grant barely heard the woman, his gaze on Mona as Sam led her off the dance floor and sat her in a nearby empty chair, his hands resting on her arms.

"I'm Tacey Reese." The tall, sandy blonde held out her hand. "And you are—?"

Grant's hands clenched into fists.

Tacey's smile twisted. "Obviously not interested." She stepped out of his arms. "Well, thanks anyway."

Grant dragged his gaze from Sam and Mona and glanced down at Tacey as if seeing her for the first time. "I'm sorry, it's just…"

"You've got a thing for her?" She tipped her head toward Mona. "I get it. You don't have to entertain me. But you might consider this…sometimes dancing with another woman makes the one you want take more notice." Tacey's brows rose in challenge.

"It's the least I can do." Grant held out his hand, forcing his attention away from his partner and the woman he'd lost to his own stupidity. "Care to dance, Tacey Reese? I'm Grant Raleigh, the cowboy with the bad manners."

Her jaw dropped. "*The* Grant Raleigh?"

"Afraid so."

"I'd love to dance with you, even if you only have eyes for another woman. Anything to get to two-step with a rodeo star." She raised her arms and stepped out on the floor. "Ladies, eat your heart out."

Grant had to laugh. Tacey had a sense of humor and didn't take his lack of interest in her personally.

"So what's the story?" Tacey asked.

"What story?"

"You and that other woman. What's up with her? Did she break your heart?"

Grant stumbled, stepping on Tacey's foot. "Sorry."

Tacey didn't miss a beat, limping a little, but determined to get the scoop out of him. "I take that as a yes. I thought you were married? Is that it? You fooled around with that other woman when you were married? Are you still married?" She backed away from him and would have pulled out of his grip had he not tightened his hand around her waist. "Just so you understand, I make it a rule not to mess with married men."

"It's a long story. And, no, I'm not married, nor was I when I met…that other woman."

"I have time and I'm a sucker for a sad story. You want to blow this joint and find a cup of coffee?"

With Sam leading Mona back onto the dance floor and holding her close to his body, Grant couldn't stay and watch as the woman he loved fell for a better man than he was. "I'm not jumping in the sack with you."

"And I'm not asking you to." Tacey smiled at him. "But I might ask you to buy me that cup of coffee."

"Let's go." Grant grabbed her hand and led her toward the exit before he went to war with his new partner over the same girl he'd left his old partner over.

At the truck stop on the edge of Temptation, where two major highways met, Grant sat with a perfect stranger who seemed hell bent on dragging out his life history over a cup of really bad coffee that resembled stump water.

Tacey led off with, "You and Dalton Faulkner used to be partners, right?"

Grant nodded. "Dalton and I go way back to when we were in high school, doing local rodeos. We teamed up then."

"Wow, all the way back to high school." Tacey shook

her head. "And you two aren't even talking now, from what I hear."

"You know a lot about the circuit." Grant's eyes narrowed. "Are you a reporter or something?"

She shook her head. "No, but I keep up with the cowboys and rodeo news. There's something about a cowboy who's tough enough to stare a bull in the face and still get on it that makes my heart go pitter patter."

Grant chuckled. "Tacey, I don't know why you're hanging out with me when there's a saloon full of cowboys who'd love to know they make your heart go pitter patter."

Tacey grinned. "Like I said, I'm a sucker for a sad story. So, let's hear it. You and Dalton were partners. What happened that made you two split?"

"I knew Dalton could be a player, but I trusted the man with my life on more than one occasion. I just shouldn't have trusted him with Mona."

"Mona is her name?" Tacey nodded. "Go on."

Grant took a deep breath into his constricted lungs and continued. "She'd met Dalton first, and he'd swept her off her feet. When I came into the picture I was smitten by the pretty brunette with her sunny smile and playful laugh. But she was with Dalton. At least until Dalton decided to share." His groin tightened in remembrance of that first night he, Dalton and Mona had been together. Never in his life had he considered making love to a woman with another man in the same room, much less both of them making love to her, until he'd been on the circuit with Dalton for a year. His partner had introduced him to the possibility at the last rodeo, with a buckle bunny who'd been more than willing to teach them the ropes of a ménage.

"Let me get this right…you shared the girl?" Tacey leaned forward, the color in her cheeks heightened. "As in, you both had your wicked way with her?"

"I know it sounds so wrong, but at the time it felt right. And she was all for it."

Tacey's cheeks grew pinker and she fanned herself with her napkin. "Gets me horny just thinking about it. Two hot cowboys. I'm about to cream my panties. Do you realize that's every woman's wet dream?"

Grant shifted in his seat. "Sorry."

"Oh no, go on." She dragged in a deep breath, her chest rising, her nipples tight little buds pressing through the rib-knitting of her T-shirt. "Please."

"I made a promise to her that I'd be back for her at the end of the season. That our relationship wasn't over just because we left Temptation."

"And you didn't keep your promise." Tacey stared at him, her gaze open, honest, demanding honesty out of him.

"No." Grant glanced down at his hand holding the coffee mug. "At the next town, Dalton moved on to the next woman, completely blowing off what the three of us had shared. But I had every intention of keeping my promise, with or without Dalton."

"What happened?"

"Our wild past caught up with us. The woman we'd shared at the stop before Temptation showed up, claiming she was pregnant. She demanded that one of us marry her or she'd take her problem to the press. Dalton laughed at her and told her to prove it."

"And she did?"

"Yeah, she got a DNA test. It was Dalton's baby, all right."

Tacey gasped. "Did he marry her?"

"When I confronted him with the truth, he refused."

"Jackass." Tacey sat back against the seat. "What happened to the pregnant woman?"

Grant pushed a hand through his hair.

"You stepped up to the plate." Tacey snorted. "What about Mona? How did you let her down?"

"It's not one of my prouder moments."

"Oh, you *didn't* break it off in a text or over the phone, did you?"

He nodded. "I couldn't get back to Temptation, not in the middle of the season and I couldn't marry the woman without first letting go of the one I loved."

"Makes sense, but by the phone?" Tacey shook her head. "Not cool."

"The next time she called, I told her I'd been wrong. We had no future and she shouldn't wait around for me because I wouldn't be coming for her."

Tacey winced. "Harsh. You made her hate you so that she'd get over you quicker?"

"I didn't want her to come looking for me. I thought it would be best to break it off completely." Grant glanced out the dark window of the truck stop. "I married Desiree in front of a Justice of the Peace so that she wouldn't have to raise the baby alone."

"You didn't love her."

"No, but I promised to make a good life for her and the baby. They didn't deserve to suffer because Dalton was a dick."

"But you were still partners in the team roping. How did that work?"

"Before all this happened, we were at the top of our game, as far as team ropers went. No one could beat our time and the sponsors wanted us on every ad." Grant's lips thinned. "When Dalton refused to own up to his responsibility, our partnership took a hit. I lost respect for him and it showed in our work. But we had sponsors to live up to. I couldn't quit."

"Until?"

"Desiree came with us. I don't have a home to go to, so she was stuck living out of a trailer. She was okay with that. The press got wind of it and painted it up to be a whirlwind, fairytale romance. She enjoyed being in the spotlight and played it up, happy to get in front of every news camera she could. I didn't care about much of anything back then."

Tacey sighed. "Because your heart was hurting?"

"I'd settled in for the long haul, making the best of the situation and trying to make a good life for my wife and her coming baby. But one night when I went out for groceries, I came back to find Dalton in bed with Desiree. She was about four months along, just starting to show."

"Ouch." Tacey touched a hand to his. "Dalton was a dick."

"If I thought he cared about her, I might have let it

slide, but he didn't. He took what he wanted and left the rest for others to clean up."

"Remind me to steer clear of Dalton Faulkner."

"Trust me. He's not someone you want to fall for."

"What happened with your wife?"

"She miscarried."

"Intentionally or was it an act of God?"

"Whatever it was, she wasn't sticking around. She signed divorce papers and hopped in bed with the next cowboy who'd have her."

"Wow." Tacey raked her hands through her long blonde hair. "I said I liked a good sob story, but…wow. Yours is one of the saddest I've heard in a while."

"Yeah, and now my new partner is falling for the woman I came back for."

Setting her cup on the table, Tacey pushed back her chair. "Finish your coffee, you're coming home with me."

She was pretty and nice and her nipples were still budded and poking against her shirt, but she wasn't Mona. "I told you, I'm not sleeping with you."

"I know. Again, I didn't ask you to. You share a trailer with your partner, don't you?"

"Yeah." Grant's eyes narrowed. "So?"

"What if your partner brought your sweetheart home with him?"

Grant's chest tightened. He hadn't thought of that.

Tacey shook her head. "Look, I'm not going to jump your bones or make you get me pregnant so you'll marry me. I'm just trying to help you out. All the hotels or B&B's in the area are full with the rodeo in town.

Either you sleep in your truck or you come home with me. I don't care." She stood. "What's it going to be, cowboy?"

Maybe he was the dumbest cowboy in all of Texas and more than likely he was making yet another huge mistake, but he stood and followed Tacey out the door.

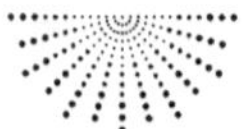

ona almost cried as she watched Grant leave the saloon with the tall, athletic blonde. Before the song was over, she stopped and gazed up at Sam. "I have to get back to work."

"Are you sure you're okay?" Sam held on to her hand a moment longer. "You seem shaken by your fall."

"Yeah, I guess I'm embarrassed. I'll get over it. Thanks for helping me up. You didn't have to, not after I slapped your face."

He grinned, rubbing his chin with his free hand. "I deserved it."

She turned to walk away, but he still held her hand.

"Let me have a second chance with you, Mona." He pulled her back to him. "Go out with me tomorrow night."

"Sorry, I'm working the night shift here at the Ugly Stick all week." She didn't let him know that she could have a three-hour gap between the time her shop closed and when she was due at the saloon.

"Then let me take you to lunch," he persisted.

"I have a day job and I work through lunch."

"Coffee?" He squeezed her hand. "I promise, I won't try to kiss you…unless you want me to."

Mona sighed. "You don't give up, do you?"

"Not when I want something really bad. And I want to see you again."

She glanced at the cowboys sitting around the tables she was supposed to be serving. Audrey had picked up her slack, but she'd need to give one of the other girls a break soon. "Okay. Coffee. Ten in the morning at PJ's Diner."

He tugged her hand, pulling her snug up against him. "Until then." Instead of trying to kiss her again, he cupped her cheek and brushed his thumb across her lip. Then he let go and walked away.

For a long moment, Mona stood in the middle of the floor, more touched by his simple gesture than any kiss she'd ever received.

From what she could tell, Sam Whitefeather was a nice guy. The kind of guy she should go for. Not the Daltons and Grants of the world who had no more respect for her than a buckle bunny following the rodeo cowboys from town to town.

Audrey and Bunny converged on her as soon as she made it back to the bar. "Was that him?" Bunny asked. "Was that Grant Raleigh you dissed?"

Mona dragged in a deep breath. "Yes."

"I loved that you didn't take his hand and took his partner's instead."

Mona frowned. "What do you mean?"

"I asked around. The guy you danced with is Sam Whitefeather, Grant Raleigh's team roping partner. Way to show Grant what you think of him."

Mona leaned against the bar and closed her eyes. Was fate playing a really bad trick on her? Hadn't she been hurt enough by Grant and Dalton already?

Bunny laid a hand on her arm. "Mona? Are you okay?"

"I'm peachy." She pushed away from the counter, grabbed an empty tray and turned toward the sea of cowboys, blinking away sudden tears washing over her eyes.

"I thought you said you were over Dalton and Grant." Bunny slipped an arm around her waist.

"I am." She was certain she was over Dalton, but seeing Grant had triggered all her heartache in one solid lump weighing heavily in her gut.

"Then why not a have a little fun with Grant's new partner?" Bunny made it all sound so easy.

"I'm having coffee with him tomorrow morning."

Bunny clapped her hands. "That's great."

"I agreed before I knew he was Grant's new partner. Now, I don't know."

"Go. What will it hurt? It's only coffee, not a lifetime commitment."

Her friend was right. Coffee wouldn't change her life forever.

SAM LOOKED around the bar for Grant. When he didn't find him, he figured the man had gone on without him. Rather than sit at his table alone, Sam returned to their trailer only to find it empty. Too keyed up to lie down and sleep, he drove around Temptation and found himself back at the Ugly Stick Saloon around closing time. Cowboys piled into their trucks, some too drunk to drive, designated drivers picking up the slack. The local sheriff's department was on hand, offering rides to those who didn't have designated drivers, to make sure everyone got home safely.

Nice. Sam liked that the townsfolk cared enough to ensure the safety of their own as well as their visitors. It was the kind of town he could see himself living in. Grant had talked about giving up the rodeo and settling down on a ranch and raising cattle and horses. He'd offered to go into a partnership with Sam, if he was interested.

Sam was good with that proposal. He had money set aside for his sister's college tuition and enough to put a good down payment on property.

Was this the town he wanted to settle in?

An image of Mona dancing on the bar, smiling and laughing, flashed through his mind. The fire in her eyes as she'd slapped his face for kissing him had only made him want to kiss her more.

Speaking of Grant, where was the man? Had he found a woman to go home with? Maybe the tall blonde drink of water he'd danced with?

Sam grinned. *About time.* The man had been celibate

since he and Sam had become partners. He deserved to find someone who made him happy.

Which was why Sam hung out at the Ugly Stick at closing time. He told himself it was to make sure Mona left without being accosted by some of the rowdier drunks. Truth was, he wanted to see her again.

She exited through the back door and strode to a red, vintage Camaro sports car and fumbled for her keys.

Sam watched from his truck, feeling a bit like a stalker. He almost turned his truck around and left, but something made him wait.

A big man in a dark cowboy hat lurched out of the shadows and made for where Mona stood beside her car, digging through her purse.

Warning bells went off in Sam's head and he opened his door to get out of his truck.

The man was on her before Sam could get to her, wrapping his arm around her neck.

Mona dropped her purse, grabbed the man's arm and tucked her body, throwing the hulk of a human over her shoulder.

He landed on his back, hard. Still holding his arm, Mona bent his thumb all the way back and stared down at her attacker. "Wanna go for round two, George?"

"No, ma'am."

"Then get your ass home to your wife and don't ever attack another woman. Ever. Or I'll come after you, cut off your balls and feed them to the coyotes."

"Yes, ma'am," George moaned from the ground. "You gonna let go of my thumb afore ya break it?"

"I'm thinking about it." Finally she let go of the man and nudged him with her cowboy boot. "Go on, get out of here before I sic the sheriff on you."

The man rolled to his feet and ambled off. He climbed into a pickup and gunned the engine, kicking up gravel as he left the parking lot and hit the highway home.

Sam leaned against the side of the Ugly Stick Saloon and chuckled.

Mona spun, ready to take on her next attacker.

Stepping out of the shadows, he let her see it was him.

Instead of relief, her forehead dipped into a frown. "What are you laughing about?"

"I'm impressed." He bent to help her collect the items that had fallen from her purse when she'd dropped it. "I thought I was sticking around to rescue you should someone try to attack you as you left work. Looked more like George needed the rescuing."

"He's a dumbass too full of whiskey to be thinking, much less driving."

"Then why did you let him go?"

"Deputy Cramer is just down the road. He'll pull him over and give him a free night's sleep in the Temptation jailhouse. Why are you here? I thought you left a long time ago."

"I wasn't tired enough to sleep. And some pretty little brunette with a body that doesn't quit and an attitude bigger than her boots kept me awake."

"You'll get over it." She clicked the unlock button, her door lock popped up and she yanked open the door.

"I'm not so sure."

"Trust me. In the next town, you'll meet another girl just like me. Difference is, maybe she'll let you sleep with her. I'm not in the market for a one-night stand."

"Your sign is out and I read the fine print. *Don't kiss her and don't expect sex.*"

"Good, I wasn't sure you'd gotten the message." She leaned down to get into her car.

A woman stepped out of the back of the saloon and locked the door behind her. When she turned around, she frowned and walked toward Mona. "Mona, are you okay? This man isn't bothering you, is he?"

"I'm fine. And no, he's not bothering me. He was just leaving."

Sam tipped his hat at the woman and held out his hand. "Sam Whitefeather, I'm here for the rodeo."

"Audrey Anderson. I own the Ugly Stick."

"Nice place."

"Thanks." Audrey turned to Mona. "Want me to stay until you leave?" She shot a glance at Sam. "No offense."

He nodded with a smile. "None taken. I'm glad you care enough to see to the safety of your employees."

"I love my girls and wouldn't want any one of them to come to harm."

He raised his hands. "I'm not here to harm. I just wanted to invite Mona out for a bite to eat."

"Oh, that's nice. The truck stop is the only place open twenty-four hours a day. You can get a great country-fried steak there." Audrey smiled at Mona. "I'm headed home. Jackson is keeping the sheets warm for me."

"Lucky girl." Mona hugged Audrey. "See you tomorrow."

Audrey left and Mona started to get into her car.

Sam touched her arm. "Would you like to go with me to the truck stop for a late dinner?"

"No," Mona said, her tone clipped.

"A cup of coffee?" Sam had the feeling if he let her go, he wouldn't see her again.

"No again." She straightened. "As a matter of fact, I'd like to cancel our coffee date for tomorrow."

"Why?"

Mona chewed on her lip. "I'll be busy."

"Come on, you have to take a break sometime."

"I will."

"Just not with me."

"Right."

"Did I do something wrong?"

"Other than kissing me when I didn't want you to and now stalking me?" She shrugged. "I can't think of a thing. Suffice it to say, I don't want to have coffee with you tomorrow." With that final comment, she ducked into the car.

Sam stepped into the door to keep her from closing it. "At least tell me why."

"Perhaps you could ask your partner."

"Grant?" Sam frowned. "What does he have to do with you and me?"

"Nothing, everything. Oh, you rodeo cowboys are all alike—arrogant, full of yourselves and as useless as a bag of rocks. If I didn't see another one of you for the rest of my life it would be too soon. Just leave me alone."

She shoved him backward, slammed the door and twisted the key in the ignition. The starter clicked, but the engine didn't turn over.

Sam stood back, his arms crossed and waited for her to leave.

She turned the key again and nothing.

A smile slipped across his lips and he forced it back. It seemed fate was giving him a second chance with the lady, even if she wasn't.

Sam turned and pretended he was leaving.

Her car door opened behind him.

He kept walking, straight to his truck. When he reached it, he unlocked it and took a moment to look back.

She had the hood up on her car and was peering into the engine. She fiddled with a wire, pulled the oil stick out and shoved it back in, then slipped back into the driver's seat and turned the key again.

Click.

Sam got into his truck and waited for her to come to him.

Mona rested her forehead on the steering wheel, or maybe she was banging her head on the wheel, Sam wasn't certain from the distance.

After a while she dug in her purse and pulled out what looked like a cell phone, punched some buttons and held it to her ear.

Sam checked his cell phone. No reception in this remote part of Texas. The Ugly Stick Saloon was several miles out of Temptation, likely the only cell tower was in the town itself, leaving the countryside without reception.

Mona threw her cell phone into her purse and got out of the car, slung the strap of her bag over her shoulder and started walking.

Right past Sam's truck to the highway.

Sam started his engine and drove up beside her, sliding the window down. "Need a lift?"

"No."

"It's five miles to town."

She lifted her chin. "A good stretch of the legs."

"I hear there are coyotes in this area."

Mona gave him a *get real* look. "They won't attack humans."

"What if George comes back?"

"I'll take care of him like I did before."

"Mona, get in the truck. I can't leave you out here by yourself."

"And I really don't want anything to do with you or Grant or any other rope-throwin', bronc ridin', bullshittin' cowboy."

Sam stopped the truck and got out. "I don't know what got your panties in a wad, but not all cowboys are the same."

"No, but all *rodeo* cowboys are. You can't trust them to keep their word."

"Why not?"

"They have a girl in every town and probably one back home with a baby or two." She stood in the beam of his headlights, the light glinting off the moisture pooling in her eyes. "I'm not up for another broken heart, Sam."

"I'm not gonna give you one." He pulled her into his arms and brushed the hair back from her forehead. "I just want to take you out for a damned cup of coffee. And if it means getting slapped again, I can't help it, I want to kiss you."

He ducked his head, his lips crashing down over hers.

Mona's hands pressed against his chest for a moment, then curled into his shirt, dragging him closer.

When he drew a line with his tongue across her lips, she opened her mouth and let him in.

Sam pulled her closer, his cock straining against the tightness of his jeans.

Mona's hands slipped up around his neck, lacing through the hair hanging down below his collar. Her breasts pressed against his chest and one of her trim calves curled around the back of his leg.

He deepened the kiss, his tongue thrusting deep into her mouth that tasted of mint, so warm and wet.

When she reached between them and worked her fingers over the buttons on his shirt, he set her away from him and rested his forehead against hers. "You don't know how badly I want this."

Her fingers stilled. "But…"

"But, given the last time I kissed you and the way you feel about rodeo cowboys, doing this tonight would only reinforce your perception."

"Damn my perception. Take me now or forget about it." She grabbed the hem of her shirt and would have ripped it up over her head, if his hands hadn't stopped her.

"Not here. Not like this."

She grabbed his hand and dragged him toward his truck. "Then take me somewhere we can be alone."

"My trailer."

"No!" She stopped in her tracks. "No. Not your trailer. Your partner might be there. We'll go to my apartment."

She climbed into his truck, gave him the directions, and he set off toward Temptation, too excited to ask and ruin the mood, but wondering what the hell had changed her mind.

CHAPTER FOUR

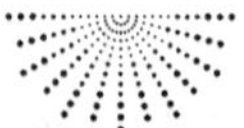

"*H*ere we are," Tacey announced.

Grant was surprised when she pulled into the parking lot near the rodeo arena where all the participants' trailers were lined up in neat rows, hay tied to their roofs. "I didn't realize you were in the rodeo as well." Hell, there were a lot of things he didn't know about Tacey. Why the hell was he going home with her?

She shrugged. "I do the barrel racing. Have been since I was a kid. But mostly around these parts. I'm from Hole in the Wall. The town on the other side of the Ugly Stick."

They passed by the trailer he and Sam shared, half of which was used to transport their horses, the other half was a fully equipped camp trailer with a stove, refrigerator, bathroom and air conditioner.

Would Sam return to the trailer with Mona, or

would he go to her place for the night? Assuming Mona was into Sam. After three years, she certainly wasn't thinking about Grant. From what he'd witnessed of her reaction to Dalton, she probably was over them both and happily single. If she chose to be with Sam, Grant had no say in the matter. He'd given up any rights when he'd called to dump her three years ago.

"I compete in barrels, but I'd like to do team roping." Tacey pulled in beside a smaller version of his own trailer. "And someday, I'd like to compete in bronc ridin'."

Grant's leg still throbbed a bit from the last rodeo when he'd landed on it wrong, in a less than graceful dismount. "It's really hard on your body."

"Yeah. But I like the adrenaline rush." She shifted into park. "Look, you don't have to stay here, if you don't want to."

His gaze shifted down the line of trailers to his own. "No, I'm good with this. As long as we understand each other."

Her lips twisted into a rueful smile. "I know. Hands off the gorgeous cowboy, he's in love with someone else. I get that a lot. You'd think I would have the pick of the litter, riding the circuit with all the men, but they seem to shy away from me." She tipped her head. "Am I that homely or intimidating?"

Grant chuckled. "Not at all. I find you very attractive. If I wasn't in love with someone else, I'd be tempted."

"Nice, but I'm not buying it." She climbed down

from the driver's seat and headed for the trailer. "It's up to you. Stay here or not."

Grant couldn't bring himself to risk Sam and Mona making love in the same trailer as he was sleeping. He hurried to catch up with Tacey and took the keys from her fingers. "I'd like to stay."

She stared up into his eyes and sighed. "Yeah, well, I'm not all that sure I can keep my hands off you. But I'll do my best." She pushed past him and climbed the steps into the trailer.

Grant followed, one last glance back toward his trailer. So far Sam hadn't shown up with or without Mona. His heart squeezed in his chest and he closed the door. Why torture himself?

Tacey pulled a bottle of whiskey from an overhead cabinet and fished in another cabinet for a cup, settling for two coffee mugs. "Want some?"

"Might as well."

She tipped the whiskey bottle and poured it into the mug, filling it halfway and handed it to him. Then she poured another for herself and lifted it in salute. "To lonely hearts."

The ceramic mugs clinked and Grant downed the whiskey in one swallow, the amber liquid burning a path down his throat.

Tacey didn't even flinch as she downed her own and smacked the mug on the counter. "You can have the bed or I can make up the kitchen table into a bed."

"I won't put you out of your bed, and I can do the conversion. We have one like this. Sam usually sleeps on it." The mention of Sam made his gut clench again.

"Knock yourself out." Tacey turned away and whipped her top off. "I'm going to get a shower. I'd ask you to join me, but it's barely big enough for one, much less two people." She turned to him, wearing her jeans and a black lace, demi-bra, her full breasts pushed up in beautiful mounds.

Grant gulped, his jeans tightening, his cock throbbing against his fly, despite his promise to himself to be true to Mona. "No worries. I'll just get to work on this kitchen table."

"I'll be right out." She turned away, unbuttoning her jeans. "There's a chocolate cream pie in the fridge if you want some."

"Pass." He told himself he should turn away and give Tacey some privacy, but he couldn't.

The barrel racer slipped her jeans down her legs, revealing the narrow strap of her thong panties disappearing between her butt cheeks.

Grant's fingers curled into fists, every cell in his body screaming to take what was offered.

Then Tacey unclipped the back of her bra and let it slide down over her arms to her fingers. She let it dangle from one of her hands, then turned, giving him a side view of her luscious breasts. "I'll only be a moment."

Before he could untangle his tongue to respond, she ducked into the bathroom and closed the door.

Big mistake. Echoed in Grant's head. If he had any sense of decency, he'd leave while Tacey was in the shower. But the sight of her long, lean body and full, voluptuous breasts had him aching to see more. Was it wrong to look, if he didn't touch?

Grant lowered the table, spread the cushions over it and scrounged in an overhead cabinet for a spare set of sheets. By the time he had the bed put together, the water shut off in the bathroom. He braced himself for when she stepped out, not knowing if she'd come out naked or what.

As he reached for his boots, he debated making a run for it, but decided against it. If he was truly in love with Mona, the temptation of Tacey would have no effect on him.

Yeah, right.

She stepped out of the shower wrapped in a short towel that barely covered all the important parts, her hair combed away from her face and dripping down her back. "Nothing like a three-minute shower to get the body humming. You're welcome to it."

"Thanks, but I had a shower earlier." He sat on the makeshift bed and pulled his boots off.

Tacey worked her way around him, dropping the towel as she reached into a drawer for a T-shirt. "Sorry. Didn't mean to give you a full moon."

Grant groaned. "If anyone ever tells you they think you're homely, tell them to get glasses." He set his boots to the side and glanced up at her, forcing himself to look at her, without lusting after her. "You're beautiful."

"Then what's it going to take to get you to make love to me?" She planted herself in front of him. "Oh, I know I said I had no expectations, but damn, you're hot and

I'm…well, I'm on fire." She plumped her breasts. "Don't I tempt you in the least?" Tacey straddled his knees and sat in his lap, her triangle of hair damp from the shower. "How about this—sex with no strings and no commitment?"

He rested his hands on her hips and dragged in a steadying breath. "I can't."

"Can't?" She tapped his crotch, a smile sliding across her face. "The body seems willing."

"Oh, I want to have sex with you. But it wouldn't be right." He lifted her off him and stood. "This is a mistake. I'd better leave."

Tacey pouted. "She must be pretty special."

"She is. And I didn't do right by her the first time we met. I can't compound the error of my ways by giving in to my baser instincts and having my way with you." He cupped her face. "No matter how very tempting you are." He stepped to the side, grabbed his boots and hat and hurried toward the door before his resistance crumbled.

"I hope she appreciates you." Tacey stood with her hands on the gentle swell of her hips. "I'm good." She tapped the side of her leg. "Strong thighs."

"I can't."

"Because you're still in love with Mona." Tacey sighed. "After cutting her off with a phone call, do you really think you have a chance to win her back?"

"I have to try."

"I'm here and now. Mona may never happen. Not after a douche-bag let down." Tacey ran her hands up her sides, plumping her breasts. "Sure you won't change your mind? I'm only in it for the sex."

Grant smiled at her. "You're pretty wonderful, Tacey. There will be a cowboy come along that will discover just how great you are."

She gave him a crooked smile. "Just not you."

"Not me."

"Mona doesn't know how good she has it. I hope she gives you that second chance." Tacey stretched, showing off her beautiful body one last time, before she shrugged, defeated. "Can't blame a girl for trying. At least save me a dance next time I see you at the Ugly Stick."

"You bet." Grant let himself out of the trailer and closed the door behind him. The warm night air did nothing to cool the raging heat inside him. If only Tacey had been Mona, he'd have danced in the sheets with her all night long. He shook his head. No. He couldn't betray her again. Yes, he was free, single and horny, but that didn't make it right. Not if he wanted to win back Mona.

Still…an image of a naked Tacey straddling his legs came to mind—an image that would be mighty hard to forget.

MONA SAT BESIDE SAM, her hands twisting in her lap. The night hadn't quite gone the way she'd thought it would. From blowing off Dalton, to dancing with Sam and falling all over herself at the sight of Grant, she felt like she was spinning out of control.

Five times on the road to her apartment, she almost told Sam to stop the truck and let her out to walk the rest of the way. She needed time to clear her head, get a grip and figure out what the hell to do.

Sam seemed to be a nice guy and he could kiss like nobody's business. Thus the reason for her being in the front seat of his pickup on her way to her apartment to get laid after a three-year sabbatical with only her vibrator to keep her hot at night.

When they pulled into the back alley behind her beauty shop, she jumped down before Sam could round the pickup and open the door for her.

He met her at the base of the steps up to her apartment.

"Look, Sam…"

"Don't worry, if you've changed your mind, I'll understand." He took her hand and carried it to his lips. "But promise me you'll have a cup of coffee with me."

His brown eyes stared down into hers, the light from the landing above making them shine.

Her knees melted and she leaned into him, telling herself she only wanted a kiss. After all, Sam was Grant's partner. Sleeping with him would only complicate everything even more.

When her lips touched his, she knew her mistake and couldn't take it back. She wanted more than a kiss and settling for less wasn't an option.

Mona opened her mouth to his tongue, accepting his thrusts, wondering what it would feel like to be beneath him, his long hard dick thrusting into her wet, aching channel. Grant had been well-endowed, his cock thick and hard. Would Sam equal up? Would he help her to forget Grant?

Her pussy creamed at the thought and she wrapped her arm around his neck, drawing him closer. Her nipples rubbed against the lace of her bra, making her want to strip it and the shirt from her back to rub those pointed nipples against his smooth hard chest.

She flipped the buttons on his shirt open all the way down to where it disappeared into his jeans and didn't stop there, grasping the top button of his waistband.

His hand covered hers. "Are you sure?"

She chewed on her lip, an image of Grant flashing through her mind. *Hell, he'd had his chance three years ago.* A surge of old anger helped her reply, "Yes."

Sam smoothed a hair back behind her ear. "You won't regret it later, and think I'm just like the other rodeo cowboys?"

"I promise."

He snorted softly. "Why don't I believe you?"

"Do you always talk this much?" She ripped his shirt out of his trousers and shoved it over his shoulders.

"One more question." He kissed the tip of her nose. "Do you always undress men in public?"

She grabbed the hem of her shirt and dragged it up over her torso and breasts and tossed it in his face. "Do you always analyze things to death?"

"Only if they perplex me." He frowned, holding her shirt in his hand. "And you perplex me."

She reached behind her and unhooked her bra. "Then analyze this." Mona flung her bra in his face and raced up the stairs. Her hand shaking, she jammed her key into the lock. What had come over her? Had she just stripped outside her apartment with a man she'd met a couple of hours ago? A stranger to her. For all she knew, he could be a nut case. Or a really nice guy she wanted to make love to her to help her forget Grant. Then she'd show him the door because he was with the rodeo, and he wouldn't be staying around when the show was over anyway.

Her pulse pounded and her breath caught in her throat as Sam ran up the stairs behind her. A twinge of guilt had her chewing her bottom lip again. Was it fair to Sam that she was using him to get over Grant?

She shoved the door open, refusing to think past her heated loins. Before she could get inside, Sam scooped her up in his arms and carried her over the threshold, kicking the door shut behind him. He was strong, his arms like steel bands around her. A shiver of excitement rippled across her body.

Why was she worried? Why was she feeling any guilt whatsoever? Grant had dumped her, married another woman within weeks and hadn't been back for three years.

With an optimistic stash of condoms in her night-stand and no commitments to anyone, Mona was a free spirit, capable of making love to anyone she damn well pleased without guilt or hesitation.

Sam didn't put her down until he reached the tiny bedroom where her queen-sized bed took up almost all of the space. He set her on her feet and ran his hands down to her waist and lower to slip into the waistband of her cutoff jean shorts.

He kissed her, his tongue tracing the line of her lips, then he dragged his mouth over her chin and down the long line of her neck to where the pulse beat like a snare drum at the base.

"You're wearing too many clothes," she whispered, pushing the button of his jeans through. She slid the zipper down and parted the fly. Before she could wonder whether he wore boxers or briefs, his cock sprang free into the palm of her hand.

Ah yes, a man after her heart. He preferred going commando.

She couldn't get the jeans off him fast enough.

Dalton had been a boxers guy. Grant preferred nothing at all, like Sam.

With Sam's jeans down to his knees and her own sliding over her thighs, why did she have to think of Grant?

Mona forced thoughts of Sam's partner from her mind and stepped out of her shorts, standing naked in front of Sam as he kicked his boots off and dropped his jeans on the floor.

He backed her up to the edge of the bed and she sat.

Sam leaned over her, easing her down to the mattress, her legs dangling off the edge. He picked up where his lips had left off at the base of her throat and blazed a trail of kisses and nibbles across her collarbone to the smooth mounds of her breasts.

Mona inhaled, her chest rising, encouraging Sam to take one of the turgid peaks between his lips.

He did, sucking it into his mouth and rolling the tip

of her nipple across his tongue. His hand slid down her ribs to the juncture of her thighs.

She widened her legs, eager to have him there. He'd captured her attention from the start with his high Indian cheekbones, swarthy skin and a chest so broad it filled the room. His smooth, darkly tanned skin and work-roughened hands were doing crazy things to her.

Mona shut out thoughts of Grant and let Sam fill her mind, body and soul. She moaned and squirmed beneath his touch, wanting so much more.

And the man gave it to her. One long digit slipped into her drenched pussy, swirling as her muscles contracted around it. Then another finger joined the first and another as he pumped in and out of her, while his lips heated her belly and found the soft mound of hair covering her mons.

Her breath hitched as he parted her folds and stroked a wet finger over the center. Mona arched her back, her fingers twisting in his hair, urging him closer.

He draped her thighs over his shoulders and went in for the clincher, his tongue snaking out to lap at her clit.

Mona's heels dug into his back and she moaned, the tension building inside, sensations tingling from her core all the way to her toes. "Now."

"Not until you're there," he whispered against her damp pussy and tongued her again, sending her rocketing over the edge. Her body stiffened and she rode the wave of ecstasy as he flicked and laved her until she could take it no more and tugged at his hair, pulling him up her body.

Sam stood, but refused to enter her. "Protection?"

"In the drawer. Hurry!" She moaned, wrapping her legs around his buttocks, the cool air doing nothing to chill her desire.

He dove for the drawer and rummaged until he found a foil packet, ripped it open and rolled it down over his engorged cock. Then he thrust into her in one long, slow stroke, filling her with his length and girth.

Mona locked her legs around his waist and pressed him deeper. "Harder," she urged.

"I don't want to hurt you." He smoothed a hand down her belly to her thatch of curls, finding and flicking her clit.

"Sweet Jesus, do it!" She flexed her legs, slamming him into her.

He gripped her hips and went at her like a jackhammer, pounding into her again and again, his huge cock burning to her center. His body grew rigid, his fingers digging into her buttocks, and he threw back his head as he rammed into her one last time.

She hit a second wave as his cock throbbed inside her. For a long moment they remained still, savoring to the last spasm the magic of making love.

Then Sam withdrew from her, peeled off the condom, tossed it in the trash and climbed into the bed beside her. He pulled her up onto the pillow and spooned her backside against him. "You're incredible."

"So are you." She lay with her back to the man, her thoughts whirling, spinning images of Sam and Grant together until she felt so dizzy she couldn't take it anymore. Mona pushed Sam's arm away and got out of the bed.

"Are you okay?"

"Yes." Then she ducked into the bathroom and closed the door behind her.

What had she just done? She could still be in love with Grant, yet she'd just had soul-shattering sex with his partner. How the hell would she dig herself out of this emotional crater?

CHAPTER FIVE

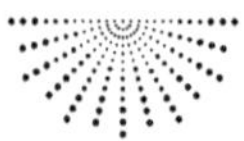

Sam woke before dawn and lay there watching Mona as the sun peeked through the window, spreading a ray of pale, yellow light over Mona's naked body.

The air conditioner hadn't kept up with them the night before and she lay on top of the sheets, her legs splayed, one draped over his, her dark brown hair fanned across the pillow, golden highlights picked up by the sun. She was an angel, her face calm, unlike the night before when she'd returned to the bed, a frown denting her brow.

He figured she was feeling scared and unsure of their lovemaking. He had set out to convince her what they'd done was not only good, but right. They'd made love until somewhere around two when Mona finally crashed in his arms, a smile on her face, worn out and satiated.

It took Sam longer to fall to sleep as he contemplated his next move with this woman. She was as skittish as a new colt. He'd have to gentle her into believing that he wasn't out for a one-night stand, and that he wasn't like every other cowboy in the rodeo, going for the buckle and moving on to the next conquest. He had dreams of settling down and building a life for himself. Once he got his sister through college and saved a little more money toward a down payment on a ranch, he planned on raising horses, cattle and kids.

As he stared up at the ceiling, sleepless, he pictured Mona as the mother of those kids. She'd be beautiful, her belly swelled with child. Never in all his adult years had he felt this drawn to a woman. And he'd only known her for one night. He shoved a hand through his hair. Why now? Why her?

Hell, he knew why. She had a body that didn't quit. The woman was beautiful and sexy, and he fit perfectly inside her.

Leaning up on his elbow, he stared down at her creamy complexion and the way her lashes made dark crescents on her cheeks. Her lips were a deep rose, full and swollen from all the kissing they'd done.

The sun rose, warming the room. Sam slipped from the bed, careful not to wake her, and pulled on his jeans and shirt, leaving the buttons for later.

Mona would have to rise soon enough and be on her feet all day doing hair at her beauty shop. Then she'd be back at the Ugly Stick that night to serve a bunch of rowdy cowboys. The woman had to have a lot of energy and spunk to last all day long and put up with the raucous rodeo crowd.

Sam grinned. He still planned on having coffee with her at ten o'clock, but he had work to do before then. He brushed her lips with a feather-soft kiss, grabbed his boots and ducked out of her apartment, closing the door softly behind him. He waited until he reached the bottom of the stairs before tugging on his boots. His truck stood where he'd left it behind the beauty shop in the alley.

A woman leaned against it, her eyes narrowed, tapping a long-stemmed red rose in her palm, like a weapon she might use on him.

"Howdy." He straightened and crossed toward her, his feet slowing when she didn't move away from his truck.

"Sam Whitefeather, right?" she asked.

He nodded. "I'm sorry, have we met?"

"No." She stuck out her empty hand. "Bunny Leigh, Mona's best friend."

Sam nodded, beginning to see why the woman had such a fierce look on her face. "I take it you're here to warn me to leave her alone."

Bunny crossed her arms. "No. I'm here to warn you not to hurt her."

"Rest assured, I have no plans in the near future of hurting Mona."

"Good. Took her three years to get over the last cowboy that waltzed into and out of her life." Bunny pushed away from the side of the truck and stood toe-to-toe with Sam. The woman was a good foot shorter than him, but for all her small stature, she gave him a helluva big I'll-kill-you look. "I'd hate to have to come after you." Bunny tapped the red rose against his bare chest. "Got it, mister?"

He held up his hands in surrender. God forbid she should use the soft petals of the rose on him. Sam fought the smile threatening to explode on his face. Now would not be a good time to laugh. Mona had a good friend in Bunny, and for that, he was thankful. Grabbing Bunny's arms, he set her away from him and stared down into her eyes. "I've only just met Mona, but I can see she's a special woman. You don't have to worry. I'll treat her with the respect that she deserves."

Bunny's brows twisted. "Respect? Respect is a given. If you're gonna hump her bones, at least don't lead her on. That's what I care about. I don't relish the idea of picking up the pieces again. It hurts me to see her in pain."

His fists tightened at the thought of someone breaking Mona's heart. "I'd like to get my hands on the guy who jacked her up."

"You don't know who it was?" Bunny's eyes narrowed.

"No. Do you?"

She opened her mouth, then closed it. "I do. But it's not my place to say. If I'm not mistaken, Mona might still have feelings for the jerk." Bunny's shoulders sagged. "Otherwise, I'd have done him some serious damage. I better get back to work. I have to get flowers together for a funeral by noon."

"Sounds depressing."

"Would be, if flowers didn't make me so happy." She

nodded toward him. "Let me know if you need any help with Mona."

"Do you always go from threatening to offering help for your friend?"

"No. Only when I see a man who might be worthy of her."

He touched the brim of his hat. "I'll take that as a compliment."

"You should, and you better live up to it." Bunny walked to the shop next door, and stopped at the back entrance before she turned back toward him. "Just don't hurt her."

"I'll do my best." Sam climbed into his truck and backed out of the alley, shaking his head. Temptation was a town where folks knew each other and stuck up for their friends. He could like it here. It got awful hot during the summer, but it wasn't cold like it was in North Dakota in the winter.

Yeah, he could like Temptation. And he could like Mona. Sam frowned as he drove off. He wondered if Bunny was right. Was Mona still mooning over someone else? It would explain why she ran hot and cold with him. Only one way to find out.

Ask.

He whistled off key as he drove back to the rodeo grounds and the trailer he shared with Grant. They had team roping later that afternoon. Sam would take care of his horse, have coffee with Mona and still have time to go over his and Grant's strategy before they were due at the arena.

When Sam entered the trailer, Grant was already awake, his eyes bloodshot, dark circles beneath them.

"Mornin', partner. You look like hell." He laughed, the joy of the night before bubbling up inside, refusing to be tamped down. "What happened? Did you go home with that woman you met on the dance floor last night?"

Grant yanked a coffee mug from the cabinet and slammed it on the counter. "None of your goddamn business."

Sam backed up a step. "Sorry, didn't mean to pry." He tossed his hat on a chair and reached for another mug. "Gonna be a nice day for a rodeo."

"Yeah, whatever." Grant poured coffee into his mug, some of it sloshing over onto his hand. He jerked it away and flapped. "Damn."

"Here." Sam pulled a paper towel off the roll and handed it to Grant. "You should put that burn under cold water."

Grant jerked his hand away from Sam, grumbling. "I know what to do."

Sam stared at Grant. "You got a bug up your butt about something? If so, spit it out."

Grant ran his hand under cold water, his jaw tight, a muscle twitching in his cheek. "I got nothin' to say."

"Good, then I'll take care of the horses while you get your shit together." Sam left the trailer, wondering what had gotten his partner all jacked up. Grant hadn't been this surly since he quit binge drinking. If he wasn't mistaken, the man was angry and frustrated. If he had left with the woman on the dance floor, had she gotten him all hot and bothered then turned him down? It was the only thing Sam could think of. He'd give Grant some room to cool off and get his game face on. Hopefully, he'd be in his right mind when they had to perform that afternoon.

GRANT HAD no one to blame but himself. He'd spent the night tossing and turning after leaving Tacey's trailer, only to get up in a foul mood with a hard-on that hurt. A cold shower and a fight with the coffee maker only made his temper worse.

When Sam showed up at the trailer with a smile and an I-just-got-laid look, that was all he could take. More than likely he'd gotten laid by the woman Grant had come to Temptation to win back. He should have felt like a heel for taking his temper out on Sam, but he couldn't. All he wanted to do was punch his partner in the face.

Unless Mona had set him straight, Sam didn't know squat about Grant's past relationship with the pretty hairstylist. Based on how obliviously happy he'd been when he came into the trailer, Mona hadn't bothered to enlighten the man.

Which could mean two things. One: Mona didn't give a shit about Grant anymore, or two: Mona was trying to get back at Grant by screwing his partner.

Either option sucked and Grant could do nothing about it. He had no rights where Mona was concerned, and busting Sam's happy bubble would help nothing. Hell, he had a rodeo event to win before he could get the hell out of Temptation. Away from Mona with the only bright side that Sam would be away from her as well.

Less than magnanimous, Grant would rather Mona went for a stranger than falling for his partner. If he couldn't have her, he didn't want someone else that close to him reminding him of what he'd screwed up and missed out on.

A few minutes later, Sam entered the trailer. "You ready to exercise the horses?"

"Yeah." Grant downed the last of his coffee and headed out. As he passed Sam, he muttered, "Sorry. Must have woken up on the wrong side of the bed."

"No worries." Sam threw a blanket over the back of his buckskin. The animal whinnied and shifted sideways, unsettled by the number of horses nearby. "Easy there, Dakota." He ran his hand along the horse's neck and scratched behind his ears, speaking softly in Lakota to him the entire time.

Did Sam treat Mona with as much care as he did his horse? Grant's gut knotted. Was Sam gentle with her in bed? Did he whisper soft words in his native Lakota to soothe her? Did Mona like it?

When Dakota stopped dancing from hoof to hoof, Sam glanced up.

Grant realized he still stood at the top of the trailer steps, his gaze on Sam.

"You want to talk about it?" Sam asked.

Grant ducked his head, his cheeks burning. Hell no, he didn't want to talk about anything. Especially what he'd been thinking. "About what?"

Sam grabbed his saddle out of a storage compartment in the trailer and slung it over Dakota's back. "Whatever's botherin' you."

"Who said anything was botherin' me?" Grant tossed the blanket and saddle over Little Joe's back. The Appaloosa stood steady, unfazed by the activity around him. Unlike his owner.

Grant wanted to confront Sam. At the same time, he didn't want Sam to know he and Mona had been a thing at one time. Sam might feel as if he had to back off Mona and let Grant have a shot at her.

Actually, that was exactly what Grant wanted, but not because of Sam's sense of loyalty. He wanted Mona to come to him instead of Sam, without Sam pulling himself out of the equation.

Thing was, she wouldn't come to him unless he showed her how he felt. She might still be under the impression he wasn't interested since that was the last word she'd gotten from him, back when he'd made the mistake of picking up Dalton's slack.

Grant cinched the girth beneath Little Joe's belly and slipped a bridle over his head, coming to a couple conclusions as he did.

If he wanted Mona back, he'd have to woo her. *She'd* have to make the decision between Sam and him. He'd tried sharing a woman before and all that had gotten him was a loveless marriage with a woman he'd only cared about long enough for a one-night stand. In the process, he'd lost the woman he'd always dreamed of marrying.

Mona would be working the Ugly Stick Saloon that

night. If he wanted time alone with her, he'd have to catch her before that. He'd stop by her shop after their event and ask her out to dinner.

"Ready?" Sam stepped into the stirrup and swung into his saddle.

"Yeah." Grant hauled himself into the saddle and followed Sam and his mount into an open field. As they passed Tacey's trailer, an image of a tall sandy-haired blonde flashed through his mind, reminding him of how beautiful she'd been standing in front of him naked.

He shifted in his saddle, his groin tightening. He couldn't think of Tacey when it was another woman he'd come back to Temptation for. That evening he'd start his campaign to win back Mona.

Bunny slipped into the Shear Safari as Mona was flipping the Closed sign to Open. "Okay, girlfriend, spill."

Avoiding Bunny's determined gaze, Mona grabbed a broom and swept the spotless floor to keep her hands from shaking. "I don't have anything to say."

Bunny grabbed the broom from her and held it still. "I saw Sam Whitefeather leaving your apartment early this morning. Don't tell me you have nothing to say." She let go and settled in the swivel chair. "I want all the delicious details."

"Sam stayed the night. It was no big deal." *Like hell.* It was a huge deal and she wasn't sure how to proceed from the hole she'd dug herself into.

"I saw how you handled Dalton last night, and I also

saw your reaction to seeing Grant for the first time. Then you shack up with Grant's partner and you're telling me it's no big deal? I don't think so, sweetie." She patted the swivel chair beside her. "Sit."

Mona dropped into the chair and buried her face in her hands. "I don't know what to do."

"Start with how you feel about Sam."

"He's nice, handsome, and…"

"Is he good in bed?"

"Bunny!"

"You know it counts, so don't get all sanctimonious on me. You're the one who told me to take a step on the wild side. And look what it got me." Bunny grinned. "Not one cowboy, but two. Cory and Jack make me happier than I thought possible."

"This is different," Mona said.

"How?"

"I was in love with Grant."

"Okay then, let's talk about that."

She shook her head. "I don't want to."

"Too bad." Bunny stood and trapped Mona in her chair. "Do you still love Grant?"

Mona glanced away. "I don't know."

"You nearly caused a mass-casualty event at the Ugly Stick when you saw him."

Her face heating, Mona cringed. "I know. That was awful and embarrassing."

"Did you fall because he made your heart turn cartwheels?"

"I guess."

"Monaaa." Bunny shook her. "Either it did or it didn't."

"Okay, it did."

"And Sam? Does he make your heart do back handsprings?"

"What's with the gymnastics references?" Mona stalled.

"Just answer my question."

Her heart fluttered, her body heating with the memories of all he'd done to her the previous night. "Yes. Damn it." She shoved a hand through her hair. "I don't need the complication. He's Grant's partner. What will Grant think?"

"That you're screwing his partner out of some kind of revenge." Bunny straightened. "And the bastard would deserve it after what he did to you."

"Shit." Mona buried her face in her hands again. "What am I gonna do?"

"Figure it out."

"How?" she wailed, flinging her arm out.

"You have to see Grant and determine whether or not he has any feelings left for you. Ask him if he came back because he realized he'd made a mistake by letting you go in the first place."

"I can't do that." Mona pushed to her feet and paced the length of the shop and back. "I just started seeing Sam. How can I go out with Grant without hurting Sam?"

"You have to, or you'll always wonder if you still love Grant."

Mona's shoulders slumped. "I knew sleeping with Sam was a mistake."

"Was it? Really?" Bunny gripped Mona's arms. "Did it feel good?"

With a sigh, she nodded. "Yes. Really good. Hell, it's been three years since I've been with a man."

"How many vibrators and batteries have you burned through?"

"Too many to count. But I don't really know Sam. Last night could have been nothing more than lust."

Bunny wrapped her arms around Mona and hugged her. "Sweetie, you owe it to yourself to confront Grant. If you still love him, you'll have a better understanding of what your choices will be."

"What if he doesn't love me back, like before?" Mona curved her arms around her friend and pressed her face into Bunny's neck. "I couldn't take being rejected again."

"Then you'll have Sam to ease your heart."

"What if I end up loving both of them?"

Bunny smiled. "They're partners, maybe they'll consider sharing you, like Cory and Jack share me."

Mona chewed on her lip. "I don't know. It didn't work out for me last time. I lost both of them." She snorted. "Though losing Dalton wasn't a big loss. Where Grant at least called and blew me off, Dalton didn't even bother."

"Dalton's a jerk. But what makes Grant any better? He blew you off too."

"I don't know. Something in his face last night made me think he regretted it."

"Yeah, could have been gas."

Mona's lips pressed together. "Thanks. You're making me feel so much better."

"So what's it gonna be?" Bunny pushed Mona to arm's length. "Are you going after Grant to see if there's any spark left, or are you gonna sit back and always ask yourself *what if?*"

Mona closed her eyes, her head spinning with the possibilities. "Sam was really good."

"Then screw Grant."

"But I loved Grant, and I don't know if I love Sam. It's too soon to tell."

"Honey, you're single, pretty and over twenty-one. Get out there and have fun. Things will land the way they land, if you give yourself permission to jump in."

Mona sucked in a deep breath and let it out slowly. "Okay. I'll test the waters with Grant and see if they're still warm."

Bunny clapped a hand to her back. "That's my girl. Stick your neck out there. All you've got to lose is your dignity. And I think that's way overrated where love's concerned."

Mrs. Frantzen, Mona's first customer of the day, stepped through the door.

"Duty calls, sweetie." Mona hugged Bunny and smiled at her customer. "Good morning."

And the day began with a knotted stomach, a temporarily satisfied itch and a host of possibilities.

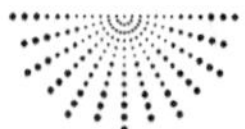

Sam tossed his saddle into the storage bin, brushed Dakota and ran inside the trailer to wash up. Ten o'clock was fast approaching and he wanted to meet Mona for coffee. He hoped she remembered.

After running a quick comb through his hair, he slipped into a clean shirt and hurried for the door, grabbing his cowboy hat from the hook on the wall.

Grant met him at the bottom of the stairs. "In a hurry?"

"I promised Mona I'd meet her for coffee this mornin' at ten."

His partner's jaw tightened and he stood back as Sam dropped down out of the trailer. "We need to be in place by one o'clock."

"I'll be back by eleven thirty."

"Good." Grant threw his brush into the storage area.

As Sam climbed into his truck, Grant threw over his

shoulder. "Careful you don't lose your concentration. Today's the big day."

"I won't lose mine." Sam shot a look at Grant. "Question is, will you?"

"I'm good." Grant's lips thinned. "And Sam…"

"Yeah." Sam jammed the key into the ignition and paused, waiting for Grant to continue.

"We've got five more stops on this rodeo circuit before we're done."

"I know."

"Just don't want you to get hurt."

"I won't." Sam twisted the key and the diesel truck's engine roared to life, drowning out any further conversation. He leaned out the window, a grin spreading across his face. Danged if he wasn't happier than a pig in a sty. "I really like her. She's different."

When he shifted into reverse, he could have sworn Grant muttered, "I know." He looked back at his friend and partner, but Grant had already turned away.

This was Sam's first Tri-County rodeo in Temptation, Texas. It wasn't Grant's. Did Grant know Mona from the last time he'd been there?

Sam made a mental note to ask him when he got back. Or maybe he'd ask Mona. In the meantime, he had a coffee date with the woman. His foot slammed the accelerator as soon as he pulled out on the highway. Ten minutes later he parked in front of the Shear Safari Hair Studio, his palms damp, his heart racing like a teen on his first date.

All because he was going to see Mona. What was it he found so interesting about her? Sure she was sexy and great in bed, but what else? She didn't take any guff from randy cowboys, she liked to dance and have a good time. Working at the Ugly Stick Saloon built character, and she never failed to smile at her customers. Yeah, she was special and Sam wanted to get to know her a whole lot better.

This was the first time since he'd left North Dakota, hell, the first time he'd *ever* considered dating a woman more than a couple casual dates or one-night-stands. He'd been too busy earning money to put his sister through school. Now that she needed him less and less, he could pursue a real relationship.

He stepped through the glass door into the shop, an acrid scent stinging his nostrils even before he could open his mouth to say hello.

"Have a seat, Charli, I'll be just a minute," Mona called out from around a corner.

Sam heard the sound of running water and voices, one of them Mona's. A minute later, a woman wearing a towel on her head emerged from behind a wall, followed by Mona.

Sam scraped off his cowboy hat and grinned. "Hey."

Mona's eyes widened and a smile graced her lips. "Oh, it's you." She blushed, her cheeks a pretty rosy hue.

"Wowza," the woman said. "You two know each other?"

"Uh, yes, we do." Mona waved a hand toward Sam. "Sam, this is Lacey Lambert. Lacey, Sam Whitefeather."

"*The* Sam Whitefeather? Of the Sam and Grant roping team?"

Sam nodded. "That would be me."

Lacey patted her towel turban. "Dang, he's a hottie. Where'd you hook up with him?"

Mona patted the swivel chair and Lacey sat. "At the Ugly Stick Saloon last night."

"Lordy!" Lacey fanned herself. "If I didn't have a hot cowboy of my own…"

"Oh hush. You know you're crazy about Nick."

"Yeah, but Sam…" Lacey's gaze raked him from top to toe and she smacked her lips. "Yum."

Sam chuckled. "Thanks. I think."

"Are you here for a haircut, or to see this sexy hairdresser for something more exciting than a trim?" Lacey grinned. "Maybe a shave with her sitting in your lap? Naked?"

Mona gasped, her cheeks flaming. "Lacey! I just met the man."

"Sorry." Her smile remained, appearing anything *but* sorry. She patted the swivel chair beside her. "Sit."

"You don't have to sit," Mona said. "Ignore Lacey, she's always thinking of sex. Why did you come by?"

He nodded toward the clock. "It's ten and I thought we were going for coffee."

Mona slapped a hand over her mouth, then ran her fingers through her hair. "That's right. I forgot all about it after last n—" She bit down on her lip, her eyes rounding. "After I got to work this morning," she added a little too late.

Lacey stared from Mona to Sam and back. "Holy crap, you two did the nasty last night, didn't you?" She practically bounced in her seat.

"No, no." Mona's face was scarlet by now. She laid a hand on Lacey's shoulder. "It's not like that."

"Oh, honey, I know that look. I've seen it on my face too often in the mirror. You got lucky." She reached out and clapped Mona on the back. "Now isn't that just great?" Lacey leaned back in her chair and shoved the towel off her head. "Hang on to your belt, Sam. She'll be ready to go as soon as she trims off the dead ends."

Mona was shaking her head. "I'm sorry, Sam. I have another appointment coming in—"

The bell over the door jangled, announcing the arrival of another patron.

"Mona, honey." A pretty woman with pale blonde hair burst into the shop. "I know I'm a bit early, but since I got ready early, I thought I'd rather sit around your shop than at home. Connor's at work and I was lonely for some girl-talk."

Grant recognized her as one of the waitresses from the Ugly Stick.

"Hey, Charli." Mona's lips twisted at Sam, and she turned to the latest customer to enter. "Sure, come on in. We have plenty of girl-talk to spare."

Lacey giggled. "And how. Mona's gettin' some."

Mona's eyes rolled toward the ceiling. "Really, Lacey?"

Charli's brows rose. "That's juicy. With who?" Her gaze shifted to Sam. "Him?" She squealed and hugged Mona. "I'm so happy for you."

Feeling a little like he was a meaty steer being eyed for choice cuts, Sam winked at Mona, hiding his disappointment over missing out on their coffee date. "You're busy. I can come by at lunch, if you're not busy."

She shook her head. "Sorry. I just made a lunchtime appointment. I don't have another break until around three."

"I'll be at the rodeo competin' about then." He fiddled with the brim of his hat. "Guess I'll see you at the Ugly Stick tonight."

Mona sighed. "I'll be there. We can talk then."

Sam took her hand and raised it to his lips. "Until then." He'd rather have kissed her lips, but with two customers waiting, he didn't want to embarrass her or have his performance graded. He spun on his boot heels, plunked his hat on his head and stepped out into the warm Texas air, the bell over the door jangling at his exit.

He'd gone all of two steps when the bell rang again.

"Sam."

His heart stuttered then raced ahead as he turned back.

Mona walked toward him, a comb in one hand as if she didn't realize it was there.

In a movement as natural as breathing, he swept her into his arms, his lips crashing down over hers.

Mona gasped, her mouth opening wide enough his tongue slipped inside to caress the length of hers. His hands circled her waist, drawing her close until her hips fit tightly against his, the ridge of his cock pressing hard against the denim of his fly.

She wrapped her arms around his neck and clung to him.

After what felt like an eternity, or maybe only a second, he finally broke the kiss and pressed his forehead to hers. "I missed you."

"You did, huh?" With a shaky laugh, she leaned back her head and stared up into his eyes. "It's only been a few hours, and you barely know me."

"I feel as if I've known you forever."

"Oh yeah?" Her gaze fell to where her fingers fiddled with the buttons on his shirt. "What color are my eyes?"

"Brown."

"Good guess." Her lips twitched, making Sam want to kiss her again. "What's my favorite color?"

He said the first thing that came to his mind, "Blue."

Her hand splayed across his chest. "Wrong. What's my favorite football team?"

"The Dallas Cowboys."

"Nice try, but wrong again." She looked up at him. "See? We barely know each other. How can you miss me already?"

"I don't know. Since I left this morning, I couldn't wait to see you again." He gripped her arms. "I *want* to know you like I've known you forever." He pressed a kiss to the tip of her nose. "When can I see you outside of the Ugly Stick Saloon?"

"I don't know." She chewed on her bottom lip.

"When *will* you know?" he urged, his fingers tightening on her arms.

She glanced down at her shoes for a moment as if struggling with the answer. Finally, she sighed. "Ask me again tonight at the Ugly Stick."

"I'll be there." He kissed her again, drawing her close until her breasts flattened against his chest.

This time, she pushed away. "I have to go."

Reluctantly, he let go. "I'll see you tonight."

If he wasn't mistaken by the way her eyes flared and her cheeks flushed, she'd been excited when she'd first seen him. Though she'd put him off until that night, there was hope.

Sam tipped his cowboy hat to the back of his head and grinned. Yup, it was gonna be a good day and an even better night.

NEAR NOON, Grant ran his fingers through his hair for the hundredth time and stepped out of the trailer. As soon as Sam had left that morning, he'd yanked out his phone and made an appointment with Mona to have his hair cut, giving her his middle name instead of his first name.

She'd asked if he'd prefer to have a barber do it and gave him the name of the only barber in town.

He'd declined, insisting on her and a lunch appointment, claiming he had to get back to work. Feeling guilty for lying by omission, he justified it by telling himself she might have turned him down flat had she known it was him, and he wanted a chance to see her no matter what the outcome was.

"Hey, cowboy, you're all dressed up for someone competin' in a few hours." Tacey strolled by, her jeans neatly pressed, a clean pale blue tank top exposing slim, well-defined arms and a narrow waist. She wore a cowboy hat and her sandy-blonde hair had been twisted into a long thick braid hanging down her back. Her clear blue eyes shone in her clean sun-kissed face.

Grant's groin tightened as an image of her plumping her full breasts slipped into his mind. "Hi, Tacey. I don't have to be in the ring until two. What about you?"

"I'm clear for the day. I'm not on until tomorrow." She dug her hands into her back pockets and rocked back on her heels. "Got plans for lunch?"

"As a matter of fact I do."

She nodded. "Really?"

He glanced away. "Yeah, with *her*."

Tacey reached out and patted his arm. "Well, I hope you get what you want out of lunch. Is this the first time you've seen her in a while?"

"Yeah."

"Best thing you can do is not push too hard. A girl likes to be courted, wooed and made to feel special."

He smiled at the cowgirl. "Why are you helping me?"

She lifted a shoulder. "I don't know. Maybe I like you enough to see you happy."

"Thanks." He turned toward his truck.

"Grant?"

He swung around.

She pulled her hat from her head and slapped it against her thigh. "If things fall through, you know where to find me."

"Again, thanks." He tipped his hat and climbed into the truck, thinking about Tacey, not Mona. Here she was offering advice to him on how to get another girl and following up with an offer to be second-choice.

The woman was sexy in a girl-next-door way, and she had a big heart to want to help him with Mona. Tacey deserved to be a man's first pick.

As Grant drove away, he glanced in his mirror. Tacey still stood where he'd left her, her long slim legs looking even longer in the tight-fitting jeans, the sun glinting off her hair, making it lighter, like a golden halo.

He stopped at PJ's Diner and collected the picnic lunch he'd ordered over the phone, then he drove down Main Street to the Shear Safari. The last time he'd been there, Mona had been renting a booth from an older stylist. According to Audrey at the Ugly Stick, the older stylist had retired and Mona now ran the business.

The sun beat down on him hot and bright. He tipped his cowboy hat lower on his forehead and stepped through the door, carrying the brown paper bag with their lunch inside, a bell overhead announcing his entry.

It took several moments for Grant's eyes to adjust. Everything inside the shop appeared dark after being out in the bright, sunlit day.

Mona looked up, a comb in one hand, a can of hairspray in the other. She squinted and smiled. "Sam? Is that you? Can't tell, the sun's really bright behind you." Redirecting her attention to her customer, she lifted the woman's hair with the comb, fluffing it, then she aimed the can of spray and gave the style a light misting. "I thought I told you I'd talk to you later tonight. I have a customer during lunch."

A sharp pain knifed through his heart. She'd arranged to meet Sam later.

Grant pulled in a long breath and let it out before speaking. "I'm not Sam. I'm your next customer."

Her hand stilled and the comb slipped from her fingers, clattering against the tile floor. "Grant?"

"Love the cut, Mona. All us girls need to look our finest for rodeo week at the Ugly Stick. The better we look, the better the men tip." The woman in the chair winked at Grant. "Don't mind me, I'm done here." She dug in her purse, pulled out a wad of bills and laid them on the counter in front of her. "Put me down for six weeks from now, same day, same time."

"I will," Mona said, her voice fading off. "Thank you, Libby. See you tonight at the Ugly Stick?"

"Absolutely. We'll need all the help we can get to handle the rodeo crowd." Libby nodded at Grant as she passed, her gaze taking him in with one long sweep of her eyes. "Nice. I hope to see you there too."

Mona frowned. "And what would Mark and Luke think of that comment?"

She shrugged. "I don't know, why don't you ask them tonight? They promised to be there to help out." Libby winked at Grant and blew a kiss toward Mona. "See ya tonight, honey."

The doorbell jangled and Libby disappeared, leaving Grant alone for the first time in three years with the woman he'd dreamed about all that time.

Mona set the hairspray down, retrieved the comb from the floor and grabbed a broom. "You can sit in the other chair while I sweep up this hair."

Grant set the bag on the counter. "I didn't come for a haircut, but I'd be glad to pay for it anyway."

The sweeping stopped and she stood with her hands resting on the top of the broom handle, her face guarded. "Then why did you come?"

"I brought you lunch and wanted a chance to talk to you. To explain."

She turned away and started sweeping again, only faster this time. "You have nothing to explain. And if you're not here for a haircut, I'm going out to lunch."

He reached out and caught her arm. "You don't have to eat the lunch I brought, but please hear me out."

"You said it all the last time I heard from you over the phone. What was it you said?" She tipped her head and stared off into the distance. "'It's over. We have nothing in common. Don't wait for me to come back, because I'm not going to.'" She nodded, her bottom lip trembling slightly. "Yeah, that about summed it up." With a slight jerk, she freed her arm. "I haven't changed, so what's the use in dredging up old memories?"

"I was wrong," he blurted, not exactly the way he'd planned. Mona had every right to be angry with him and he'd expected that. "After we left here, something else came up. I wasn't sure I'd ever be back and I didn't want to leave you hanging. It wasn't fair to you."

"So you dumped me over the phone to spare my feelings?" She rolled her eyes. "Classy. And so thoughtful."

Grant scraped the hat off his head. "Look, Mona, not a day has gone by that I haven't thought of you and all I left behind."

"Funny, I've barely thought of you or Dalton in the past three years."

His lips thinned. "I don't have anything to do with Dalton anymore. And I can't begin to tell you how sorry I am that I left. You deserved better."

"Yeah, better than a phone call." She tipped her head back and stared into his face, her eyes suspiciously moist. "So you've said your piece and you don't want a haircut. What's keeping you?"

"I want a second chance."

She stared at him like he'd grown a second head. "You want what?"

"A second chance to prove to you that I really do care for you."

"You cared enough to leave the Ugly Stick Saloon with another woman last night."

So she *had* noticed. "I did, but I didn't sleep with her. I wouldn't when it was you who's been the only woman on my mind."

"What happened to your wife?"

He hesitated, the truth too long and complicated. "We divorced soon after we were married. I never loved her."

Her lips twisted. "Convenient. And it only proves to me you have a problem with commitment."

"Not with you." He captured her hand. "Please, give me another chance?"

Anger flared in her blue eyes and she opened her mouth. Then she clamped it shut and closed her eyes.

Grant's belly knotted. "Should I take your silence as a no?"

"No."

"No about the silence or no you won't give me a second chance?"

The tension left her shoulders and she opened her eyes. "Look, it goes against my better judgment, but…"

"You're giving me a second chance." He released the breath he'd been holding. "Thank you."

She pulled her hand free of his and held it up. "I'll give you a second chance to prove to me you're not a complete ass. But we're not picking up where we left off. We're starting over from scratch."

His chest swelled and his lips curled upward. "Fair enough. We'll start over." He stuck out his hand. "Hi, I'm Grant Raleigh and you're the prettiest girl I've met. Will you go out with me?"

She took his hand, a frown pulling her brows together. After a moment, her face cleared and she gave a strained laughed. "I can't believe I'm doing this… Yes."

He'd gone into his courtship fully expecting Mona to slam the door in his face. He purposely didn't mention that he knew she'd gone out with Sam, afraid it would cause her more stress in his campaign to win her heart. Hell, Sam had clearly expressed his desire to pursue Mona, and a decent cowboy didn't horn in on another man's woman. A knot of guilt tainted his happiness that Mona had relented and was giving him a shot at mending their relationship. Nothing about coming back to Temptation was going to be easy. "Dinner tonight?"

She nodded. "My last appointment is at five and I work at the Ugly Stick from nine until midnight. Can you be here at six?"

"I can and will." He tipped his head toward the bag

with lunch. "In the meantime, I have a lunch prepared and I even brought a blanket to sit on. Would you like to go on a picnic?"

She stepped back. "Don't push this too fast."

He held up his hands. "Got it." Then he glanced at the bag. "Sure hate to waste a good lunch. PJ's does a good job."

Mona sniffed the air. "Turkey club?"

"Just the way you like it."

"Okay," she said. "But we eat here."

"Deal. I'll be right back." He spun and ran for the door, returning with the blanket and the cooler he'd left in his truck.

"We could eat off one of the manicure tables," she suggested.

"And miss out on an indoor picnic?" Grant shook his head. He wanted to do this right. "I wouldn't dream of it."

He whipped the checkered blanket out and let it drift to the floor.

Between the two of them they set out food and Grant reached into the cooler for two bottles of light beer.

They sat and he opened the bottles, handing one to her. "To second chances."

She clinked her bottle against his and they drank. Then she held up her beer. "To knowing what we *really* want."

An image of Sam's excited face flashing through his thoughts, Grant hesitated before tapping his drink against Mona's. "To knowing what we really want."

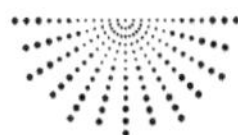

Mona sat on the checkered blanket, having forced down half a sandwich, while staring across the array of food and napkins at Grant. After three long years in which she'd sworn off men, one of the guys who'd turned her against relationships was sitting across from her, wanting a second chance.

A second chance for what? Breaking her heart again? Mona had almost showed him the door. But that spark of fire and longing that had initially attracted her to Grant was still there, and stronger than ever. A shiver rippled across her skin, her body completely aware of his sitting so close.

Grant was a handsome cowboy. Strong, confident and a winner on the rodeo circuit. If he was telling the truth and had realized his mistake, Mona could possibly have him back.

Three years of heartache was a long time. What if

during that three years she'd changed so much Grant was no longer the man for her? Sure, he was sexy and exciting, but was he the kind of man she wanted in a real, long-lasting relationship?

And what about Sam? There was a man with fresh new possibilities.

A knot of guilt formed in her belly. She'd slept with Sam last night *knowing* he was Grant's new partner. How would Grant feel about that? Mona tipped the beer bottle up and swallowed the rest in one long gulping chug.

Grant's eyes widened. "Okay. I did bring more." He reached into the cooler and uncapped another, handing it to her as she set the empty to the side.

The alcohol took the edge off her anger and nervousness over being with Grant again. She lay on her side, propping her head in her hand. "So, Grant, how's the rodeo going? What are you participating in this time?"

He dropped to his side, facing her. "Team ropin' and bronc ridin'."

"Why the new partner?"

Grant glanced at the beer bottle in his hand. "Dalton and I had a parting of the ways a few years back."

After running into Dalton at the Ugly Stick, she could understand. Dalton had always been the rowdier extrovert, while Grant had been the serious one. Three years ago, the combination of their personalities had swept her off her feet. She couldn't believe how lucky she'd been to land not one, but two gorgeous men. It had been too good to be true and she should have seen it coming. These men were on the road more months out of the year than at home. Getting involved with them had been a mistake.

Before her mother's untimely death, she'd taught Mona two things: learn from your mistakes and tigers couldn't change their stripes. So why was she jumping back into a relationship with a man who'd left her and what made her think this time would be better with Grant?

She shoved her misgivings aside and asked, "Things working out with your new team ropin' partner?"

Grant's lips tightened. "Yeah."

Ha! She'd hit a nerve. He must have seen her dancing with Sam the night before, and he might have been at his trailer when Sam returned that morning. She couldn't picture Sam as the type of man who'd kiss and tell. But then he *was* a rodeo cowboy. Who knew the extent of what ropin' partners shared over breakfast or a beer?

Mona tossed her long hair back over her shoulder, deciding to get things out in the open. "I slept with him last night." Nothing like addressing the elephant in the room. Having lost this man once, she figured if he walked out of her shop never to return, what would be different today from yesterday? She had nothing to lose. If he couldn't handle the fact she'd slept with his partner now, they wouldn't have a chance. They'd dance all around it and let it gnaw at their insides.

The muscle in the side of his jaw twitched and his full, kissable lips pressed so tightly they almost disappeared. He nodded. "Question is, did you sleep with him to get back at me?"

She swished the beer in the bottle, studying it instead of Grant's intense expression, and fell back on what Bunny had said earlier. "Well, now, that's my business. I'm a female, single and over twenty-one. I can sleep with whomever I want."

Grant set his bottle to the side, shoved the food out of the way and slid closer to her, all in a few swift movements.

Her heart hammering against her ribs, Mona couldn't look away from him. Hell, his lips were only inches from hers. Heat rippled across her body in waves, swirling like a funnel cloud to the center of her being—her throbbing, aching core. A wash of fluid warmed her pussy, and she shifted on the blanket, wondering if he could smell her musk.

Grant raised his hand to cup her face, his thumb brushing over her cheek and down to scrape across her lips. "Do his kisses leave you craving more?"

"I believe they could," Mona whispered against Grant's lips.

His hand slipped behind her neck and drew her closer until his mouth hovered over hers. He dipped in to claim her lips in a searing kiss that made her forget Sam, forget the three long years between them and forget where she was.

When he allowed her to breathe again, he asked, "Do his hands skimming across your naked body make you burn inside?"

"Umm, you bet." Mona trailed her fingers over Grant's shirt, found the top button and loosened it.

His hand slipped beneath her stretchy shirt, grazing her skin, rising to cup one full, rounded breast.

Her nipples peaked, pressing against the lace of her bra.

Grant pushed the bra upward, exposing her nipple to his rough hand. "Does he make you so crazy with passion you beg for more?"

"Oh yes, please. More." She pushed him onto his back and ripped through the buttons on his shirt. "All those thick, hard muscles make me want to climb on and ride him like a buckin' friggin' bronc."

Grant's hands cupped the backs of her thighs and followed the curve of her buttocks up beneath her skirt to her panties. Then he slid beneath the elastic and poked a finger into her tight, round anus, the pressure making her body ignite all over.

A moan rose from her throat and she ground her pussy against the ridge of his fly, fumbling beneath her to release the remaining shirt buttons, shoving it open to expose his chest. Then she grabbed for his belt buckle. "It was like an eight-second ride—surprising, exciting and much too short." She snagged the tab on his zipper and yanked it down, his cock springing free of the constraints. "So we did it again. Does that bother you?"

"No. Actually, it makes me hot." He pushed aside the strap of her thong panties and nudged her with his cock. "What about taking it slow? Starting over?"

She snorted. "We will, after this."

He shifted, raising up enough to slide his wallet out of his back pocket. From it, he retrieved a foil packet and tore it open.

"Let me." Mona took the condom and rolled it down over his thick, hard dick. Then she raised herself up over him. "Just so you know, your partner was good."

His fingers curled around her hips and he lifted her until she hovered over him, his cock poised to impale her. "Then I'll have to prove I'm better."

Her breath lodged in her lungs, she whispered, "Commence proving yourself."

He eased her down over him until she fully sheathed him.

Longer and thicker than Sam, though not by much, Grant filled her to full and lifted her off him to do it all again.

With each stroke, Mona had to remind herself to inhale and let the air out, the pleasure so intense, she almost forgot to breathe.

"Want me to slow down?" he asked, his voice strained, his face tense.

"No."

Before she could guess his next move, he flipped her onto her back and pinned her wrists above her head.

"Hold on, sweetheart, I'm gonna make you scream."

She lifted her head and glanced toward the door. "Should we lock the door?"

"Now?" He slid a hand down to her mound, parted her folds and flicked her clit with one long thick finger.

"Fuck the door," she gasped.

He laughed and leaned in, capturing her lips in a

tender but insistent kiss, sucking her bottom lip between his teeth. Letting go of her hands, he pressed her legs wide, pushing her knees up, exposing her pussy to him. "You're more beautiful than ever." He traced around her moist entrance. "So wet and hot."

"Oh, please, don't tease me." She dug her fingers into his shoulders and dragged him close. "Come inside me, now."

Grant drove into her in one long, hard thrust.

Mona dug her heels into the picnic blanket, raising her hips to meet him.

Then he was sliding in and out of her like a piston, fast and furious until she shot over the top, her fingernails scraping across his back, her voice erupting from her throat in a low, moaning scream, unlike anything she'd ever heard from herself.

In one last thrust he held her hips, burying himself so deep he had to be touching her soul, his cock throbbing. He bent to press a kiss to her lips then rose up and asked, "When is your next appointment, Mona?"

His words ripped through her haze of lust and her head jerked up. Five minutes until her next appointment. "Damn." And Mrs. Rutherford always came early —exactly five minutes early. The woman was one of the pillars of community, capable of spreading rumors—or in this case truths—like wildfire and turning others against you if she decided she didn't like you. Mona couldn't risk the bank finding out she'd been getting it on in her shop in the middle of the day. Not if she wanted them to take her serious as a business owner.

"Get up." Mona shoved hard, rolling him off her.

"Why?" He peeled off the condom, eased his stiff member inside his jeans, tucked in his unbuttoned shirt, zipped his fly and then buckled his belt in quick, efficient movements.

"My next appointment will be here any moment." She grabbed food and napkins, stuffing them into the bag Grant had brought with him. "Move!"

Grant scrambled to his feet, handed Mona the half-full beer bottles and the cooler, grabbed the corners of the blanket and scooped everything else up in one bundle and slung it over his shoulder. He held out his hand for the cooler.

Mona shoved it toward him as the door opened, rattling the bell loud enough to make her jump and hide the beer bottles behind her back. She eased backward toward the trash bin.

Mrs. Rutherford stepped in, wearing a tailored, cream-colored pantsuit, a long string of pearls and a broad-brimmed hat. "Oh, Mona, am I early?"

"Not at all, Mrs. Rutherford. Grant was just leaving." Mona's legs bumped into the bin and she slipped the beer bottles inside.

"What have you got there?" Mrs. Rutherford stepped aside as Grant strode past her, carrying the bundle and the cooler.

"No worries, ma'am. Just here cleaning up the rat problem."

The older woman gasped, her gaze shooting to the floor, her body drawing up as if she'd climbed onto a stool. "*Rats?*"

"Grant." Mona reached out and hooked Mrs.

Rutherford's arm. "He's kidding. He was just picking up some old hair rollers I'm having recycled. Weren't you, Grant?" She shot him a scathing look.

"What Mona said. No rats." With a mock salute, he plunked his hat on his head. "I'll see you at six." And Grant was gone.

Mona let out a long breath as if she'd been holding it the entire time Grant had been in the shop. Though her pulse still raced, she could now settle back into her routine and think through what had just happened. *Holy hell!* She'd had sex with Grant on the floor of her shop.

"What was that man doing in here, really? Didn't his momma raise him better than to run around with his shirt unbuttoned?" Mrs. Rutherford dropped her purse off her shoulder and stared at Mona's chest. "Um, Mona, dear, your shirt is caught in the back of your bra, your panties are showing and you smell of beer. Should I come back when you're better able to concentrate?"

Mona almost laughed and replied, *Sure and in what century would that be?*

"DIDN'T SEE YOU AT LUNCH," Sam commented as he cinched the girth on his saddle one last time before they had to head to the box for the team roping competition.

Grant dropped his stirrup, checked his rope and replied, "Had something to take care of in town."

"Not *something*." Dalton Faulkner appeared beside him, leaned against the corner of their horse trailer and stuck a toothpick between his teeth, shifting it to the side to say, "More like *someone*."

Grant shot a narrow-eyed glare at the man.

Sam glanced from his partner to Grant's ex-partner. "What do you mean?" Grant had always been honest and above-board with him since he'd sobered up and they'd gotten serious about the rodeo. "You meet someone?" Sam couldn't help but be happy for his friend. The man had been tight-lipped about his love life—the one subject he didn't share with Sam. "Was it the girl you left the saloon with last night? You two patch things up?"

"No." Grant dropped to his haunches and checked the bell boots on his horse's right front hoof. Not that he needed to, he'd checked them twice already and they were firmly in place. "Nothin' to patch up on that front. I'm not interested in her."

"No, it wasn't the pretty barrel racer he left the Ugly Stick with last night. It was someone you both know, wasn't it?"

Grant straightened. "Shut up, Dalton."

"Why?" Dalton gave Sam a wide-eyed innocent look. "Oh, wait. Is it because Sam doesn't know?"

Sam never had liked Dalton, but the man knew something Grant was keeping from him and his curiosity was piqued. "Know what?"

"Come on, Sam. We're up next." Grant ignored Dalton, grabbed his reins and led his horse toward the arena.

Sam looped his reins in his hand and set off after Grant but didn't get far before Dalton stepped in front of him.

"Saw you dancing with that pretty little beautician last night. Nice little piece of ass, isn't she?"

Sam's fists bunched. "Don't talk about Mona like that."

"She gives a really fine blowjob, if I recall." Dalton rubbed his crotch as if he was speaking from experience.

"A *real* man doesn't talk about the women he sleeps with." Grant had stopped a few steps ahead of Sam and leveled his statement at Dalton. "Don't let him get to you, Sam," he warned.

"It's true. She's got a great body and can swallow a man's dick whole." Dalton chuckled. "Isn't that right, Grant?"

Anger bubbled up in Sam. What did the jerk mean by including Grant in his remark? "Grant doesn't even know Mona."

Dalton glanced from Grant to Sam. "Is that what he told you?"

Grant blew out an angry breath. "Let it go."

"He didn't bother to tell you that not only does he know her, but he and I had her in a threesome?"

Sam's chest tightened so hard he thought it might implode. He turned to his partner. "You know Mona?"

Grant sighed. "I met her three years ago when I was here for the rodeo."

"Yeah," Dalton said. "But you're still panting after her like a dog in heat, if your trip to town at lunch is any indication."

Sam stared at Grant. "You had lunch with Mona? She told me she didn't have time today."

His fingers tightened on the reins. "I made an appointment."

"Fuck, Grant. You know I was with her last night. Why didn't you tell me? What else should I know?"

"I'm sorry, man. When you left with her, I wasn't sure I had a chance in hell. I wanted her to make her own decision without pressuring her."

"And she chose you?"

He scraped his hand over his head. "Can we discuss this after we compete?" His gaze shifted to Dalton. "And out of earshot of him?"

"What?" Dalton raised his hand. "I'm only letting your partner in on the fact you've been lying to him."

"You're a big help, like you always were." Grant's lips pressed into a tight line. "We only have five minutes to show up for our turn. I suggest we get a move on."

Sam took the lead, marching ahead of Grant, mad as hell and ready to punch his partner in the face.

Grant hurried to catch up. "I was gonna tell you."

"Yeah?" Sam didn't turn around. "When? After you sneaked off and took her to lunch? Hmm, it's been three hours since lunch. You've been with me ever since. When were you planning to tell me?"

"Actually, we didn't go out to lunch, we ate in her shop. And I was going to tell you, I just didn't know how."

"Telling the truth is that hard for you?" Sam shook his head and stopped walking to turn back toward him. "I slept with her last night. Did she tell you that?"

Grant's lips twisted. "Yeah. She did."

"Holy hell! Did you and she laugh about it too?" Sam resumed walking.

"Look, we can talk about this later and I'll tell you everything. Just understand this, Dalton brought it all up now to throw us off our game. He's messing with your head."

"And it's working." Sam ground his teeth together. "Okay. We'll talk later. Right now, we have a competition to win. I'll be damned if I let Dalton screw with our record. The bastard."

"Good. He's at the root of all that went wrong between me and Mona. I'll understand if you stay mad at me, but if you really want to be mad at someone, he's the guy. I came back to Temptation to ask Mona to forgive me."

"And seeing me leave with her last night was your way of doing it?" Sam entered the arena, leading his horse to the holding area where they'd await their cue.

"Look, I didn't know you'd fall for her the first time you met." Grant's boots crunched the gravel behind him. "Hell, you haven't known her all of twenty-four hours."

"But I *want* to know her. You had three years to get your shit together. Three years."

"I know," Grant admitted, his voice fading. "And I've kicked myself all those years."

"Well, I'm not giving up on her like you did." Sam paused at the entrance to the arena. "If you want Mona, you'll have to convince her you're worth having."

"You think I don't know that?"

Sam faced him. "Why did you leave her in the first place?"

"That's a long story. I'll tell you when we're done here."

"Damn right you will."

"And you might as well know before Dalton tells you, I'm taking Mona out for dinner tonight."

"Fuck!" Sam's hand bunched into a fist and he took a step toward Grant.

"Grant Raleigh and Sam Whitefeather, you're up at gate six!" a voice shouted through the entrance.

"This discussion is not over," Sam promised. He had a lot more to say to his partner. Waiting their turn to ride wasn't the time or place.

Sam led his horse into the maze around the area and stopped in front of the wood-slatted box of gate number six, on the right of the chute with the steer.

Grant stopped behind the box on the left.

They waited in silence for the team in front of them to go.

The steer burst from the chute. When it got to the end of the barrier rope, the horses leaped from the boxes. In eight seconds, the cowboys had the steer's head and heels roped.

Sam shook off their argument, gathered his lasso in his hand and focused on the task ahead. As he sat astride his horse, he stared across the fencing to Grant.

"Mona's special. She deserves a man who'll be there for the long haul," he called out.

Grant's lips pressed together and he nodded.

The man holding the gate of the chute took that as his cue to release the steer.

Caught off guard, Sam barely held his horse back the requisite time for the steer to reach the end of the barrier rope.

Then his horse and Grant's exploded from the boxes. Grant, the header, roped the horns and quickly dallied his rope around the saddle horn. The rope jerked taut and Grant led the horse and the steer to the left.

As the heeler, Sam charged at the steer from the rear and let loose his lasso, catching both back hooves on his first toss. He'd performed this task a thousand times, but each time was unique. The steer could dart a different direction. The header could miss the horns, the rope could bounce off a hoof. This time was perfect. As soon as he had the steer's hind legs captured, Sam's horse dug his hooves into the dirt.

Grant's horse turned toward the steer and both horses backed up until the steer's hind legs were pulled out from under him.

The official's flag waved and they released the tension on the steer, easing him to the ground.

Once they released the ropes from the steer, Sam gathered his and rode out of the arena ahead of Grant, without checking the score. Now that the event was over, his anger returned and with it, his determination to get to know the beautiful hairdresser and show her that he was the better man. It would serve Grant right for sneaking around.

He rode back to the trailer, tied his horse near the

rear and went through the routine of brushing and feeding Dakota.

Grant arrived twenty minutes later. "We had the best time."

Rather than the usual high-five and back-slapping, he went right to work on his horse, the atmosphere strained.

Sam hit the shower before Grant, finishing in less than five minutes. Grant entered the trailer, glanced at the clock, grabbed clean jeans and headed for the shower.

Stewin' in his own juices, Sam paced the short length of the trailer, wondering what to do about Grant and Mona. Before the water shut off in the shower, he had a plan.

He was going to dinner with them.

CHAPTER EIGHT

"I'll have the money to you in two weeks." Mona sighed and clicked the end call button on her cell phone. "Damn."

"That the bank?" Bunny stopped spinning in the chair in Mona's salon long enough to stare at her.

"Mr. Spillman said the real estate company wants to move on the sale of the property. I only have two weeks to come up with the additional thousand dollars or they will sell it to a man who put in a bid on it after my contingency bid."

"Holy hell, Mona. I don't want an insurance salesman moving in next to my flower shop. Who will I talk to? Who'll be there when I need a quick trim?"

"I won't let it happen. If I have to dance with nothing but a fig leaf and pasties in front of the entire rodeo of cowboys, I'll do it. I've worked too damned hard to build my business at this location, I'm not giving up on it now."

"Pasties, huh?" Bunny tipped her head. "I might have a pair you can borrow. Ones with long red tassels."

"Bunny!"

"What?" She raised her hands. "I'm just trying to be helpful."

"I need to earn cash fast." Mona grabbed her broom and swept the already clean floor. "Tonight I'll ask Audrey if I can be first in line for any requests for strippers. That's the only way I know of to get quick cash."

"You're really good. You could stand to make a couple hundred dollars in a single night if the crowd's big and drunk enough to tip indiscriminately."

"I already have a couple hundred from the past couple nights' tips. And tonight I should have maybe another hundred. If I work the rest of the week I'll have close to five hundred in tips. With the money I have saved in the bank, I only need another four hundred and I'm good."

Bunny rose from the chair and laid a hand on her arm. "Let me loan it to you."

"No way. You were just telling me last week that you were in a cash crunch yourself. If you loan me the money, you won't be able to make your bills."

"Audrey has the money to loan, let her help. I heard her offer."

Mona shook her head. "I can't. When I took over this business, I promised myself I'd do it on my own. Besides when you start borrowing from friends, it mucks up the relationship. I won't let that happen. I value your friendship and Audrey's too much to jeopardize it."

"At least keep us in the back of your mind if you run up against a time crunch. I could loan you at least a hundred without breaking my bank."

Mona hugged Bunny. "Thank you. You don't know how much you mean to me."

"I hope as much as you mean to me."

"More." Worry weighed her down, but having a friend like Bunny made her burden lighter.

"Call Audrey now." Bunny released her, grabbed Mona's cell phone and shoved it into her hands. "See if she's got a gig lined up."

Mona hit the speed dial for Audrey's personal cell phone. It rang several times before Audrey picked up.

"Mona? Please tell me you're not calling in sick. The place is going to be packed tonight and I have a special program planned for after midnight."

Her fingers clenching the phone, Mona asked, "Need any strippers?"

"As a matter of fact—"

"Count me in."

Audrey laughed. "I was just about to call you and offer you first dibs."

"I'm your gal. My timeline has moved up and I need the cash."

"You're on then. Plan on a late night."

"Thank you, Audrey." Mona hung up and let go of the breath she'd been holding. "I'm stripping after midnight."

Bunny clapped her hands. "One problem mitigated. Now, aren't you going to change for your date with Grant?"

Mona glanced down at the jeans and T-shirt she wore. "What? This isn't good enough for a man who dumped me three years ago by telephone?"

"Hell, it's too good for him. But you'll want to make sure he realizes just what he missed when he let you go. If not to get his attention, it'll make you feel better when you dump *his* ass."

Mona laughed. "You know how to make a girl feel better." Her laughter died as she thought about Sam. "I still don't know what to do about Sam."

"He was awfully cute coming out of your apartment this morning with his shirt hanging open and that fresh-from-sex smile on his face."

"He was smiling?" Mona sighed. "He was really good in bed."

"Yeah, so why are you wasting your time with Grant?"

"I don't know. I still feel all soft and squishy inside when he's near. And he still hits all my buttons when he makes love to me."

"Huh?" Bunny grabbed her arms. "And when did that happen? Sometime today? Holy hell, girl, you move fast when you make up your mind."

Mona laughed. "He brought me lunch and we had a picnic right here in the shop. And other activities…"

"You didn't say a word about that. How could you keep something that titillating to yourself? 'Fess up, girlfriend."

"You were busy. I was busy." Mona sighed. "And confused. Two men in less than twenty-four hours. I should be ashamed."

"I'd say you can't have both," Bunny said. "But that would be a big fat lie. I mean, look at me."

Mona's core heated at the thought of having both Grant and Sam at one time. "I don't know. Grant and Sam haven't been together very long. Grant might go for it, but I doubt that Sam would."

"You don't know until you ask."

"I couldn't." Mona shook her head.

"How'd you ever get with Dalton and Grant at one time?"

"Grant walked in on me and Dalton in their shared trailer. Dalton asked if Grant wanted to join us."

Bunny waved a hand. "There you go. Have sex with Grant tonight in his trailer and invite Sam to join you."

"I'm not even sure Sam knows about my prior relationship with Grant."

"Hmmm." Bunny tipped her head. "It might not be the best time to spring it on him. You might want to own up to it with Sam tonight. Cowboys don't like those kind of surprises."

"You're right. I'll tell him tonight at the Ugly Stick."

"Are you seeing Sam tonight? After you've gone out to dinner with Grant?" Bunny grinned. "Girl, when you decide to get a life, you do it with a vengeance, don't you?"

"I didn't plan it that way. For all I knew, Grant wasn't interested when I decided to sleep with Sam." Mona wrung her hands. "Oh, Bunny, am I making a big mistake? I have no idea who to choose."

"Then give them both a shake and see who raises your cream to the top."

"Bunny Leigh! Since when did you start talking such trash?"

She had the grace to blush. "Cory and Jack are teaching me to say what comes to my mind as soon as it comes. Maybe I'm not ready for prime time."

"Oh, no, honey, you're *ready*, all right."

"Then let's lock the front door, slip up to your apartment and pick the perfect dress."

"Dress?" Mona twisted the lock on the front door and faced her friend. "Who said anything about a dress? I was planning on wearing a clean pair of jeans and a T-shirt."

Bunny grabbed her hand and dragged her through the shop and out the back door and up the stairs to her apartment. "Strip."

Mona's lips quirked upward. "Only if you turn on the music."

Bunny punched a button on her cell phone, brought up her playlist and scrolled down through the titles until she smiled and selected one and turned up the volume.

The bump and grind of "Nasty Naughty Boy" by Cristina Aguilera blared through the tiny speaker, filling the little apartment.

Bunny pointed her finger and dropped her eyelids with a sexy wink. "Strip."

"This is silly." She hadn't danced to that song since her hairstyling business had started making enough money she could afford to quit stripping for Audrey's parties.

"You're the one who liked the fact that I'd worked all

day without wearing panties when the boys were trying to win me over. Put up or shut up, little girl." Bunny set the phone on the arm of the couch and grabbed the hem of her blouse. "If it helps, I'll strip with you." Her shirt came up and over her head, as she circled her hips in a figure-eight pattern.

Mona's belly tightened and her pussy creamed as her gaze skimmed across Bunny's peaches-and-cream skin, noting the narrow waist and perky breasts encased in a frilly pink lace bra.

"Honey, if we ever give up men, I'm yours for the taking." The music swirled around Mona and she couldn't help swaying her hips. The rhythm brought out the sex kitten in her.

Bunny chuckled, her hands smoothing down her breasts and lower to the button on her slacks. She flipped the button free, slipped the zipper down and let the fabric fall in a pool around her ankles. "You're on."

Mona shed her jeans first, kicking them to the side. The cooler air on her legs made her widen her stance, her hips rotating to the beat, a gush of liquid slicking her channel.

As if someone turned up the heat in the room, Mona's body burned and she couldn't shuck her shirt fast enough.

"Now you're getting into it." In her bra and thong panties, Bunny spun and dipped, her hands sliding down her body.

Mona did the same, her hands stopping at the triangle of silk covering her sex. "Damn, Bunny. If I keep this up, I'm going to come before he gets here."

"Nothing like being in the mood." She danced her way slowly across the room and flung open the closet door. "The mood to pick something sexy to wear." She plucked out a black, strapless dress that was so short, it barely covered Mona's ass.

"No, it's not right for Temptation." Mona shook her head. "What would the old matrons say if I wore that to PJ's?"

"Might get them all hot and bothered and maybe their husbands would get lucky for the first time in a month." She stared at the dress and finally hung it back in the closet. "But it's not *the* dress."

Mona closed her eyes, the music sliding over her like satin, caressing her naked skin and making her want to break out her vibrator. "You really need to turn off the song. It's getting too hot in here."

"Ah ha! This is the dress." Bunny yanked out a hanger with a pale yellow chiffon dress with an under-slip of sheer silk in the same color. It left little to the imagination and if someone really stared hard enough, they would see everything beneath it.

"I might as well go naked," Mona said. "I didn't realize just how see-through that dress was when I bought it on a crazy trip to Dallas. Hell, I bought it to wear to church on Sunday."

"Oh my, the preacher would have gotten his boxers in a knot over that. He'd have had the entire congregation repentin' for staring at the harlot." Bunny giggled at her own words. "This is the one. Not only is it simple, and at first glance, chaste, it's sexy as hell and see-through enough you'll have him so hard he could drive nails with his willie."

Laughing, Mona took the dress hesitantly, the feel of Grant's hardened cock still fresh on her mind from their short picnic lunch in the salon. Her blood thickened and her core heated to molten hot.

Bunny danced by her. "Remember, you want to show him what he's missed for the past three years."

"Yeah, but not *all* of me in public." Still, the dress felt great and sexy against the skin. Why not? "Okay."

"That's my Mona." Bunny hugged her, the lace of her bra scraping across Mona's skin. "Now hurry, or you'll keep the boy waiting."

"It wouldn't hurt him," Mona muttered. "He kept me waiting for three years."

"Oh, sweetie, I wouldn't say that to him."

"I know. Sounds pretty damned pathetic." But that's what she'd been doing. After Dalton and Grant, she'd sworn off men. Had she sworn off all men, or just Grant? None of them measured up to her expectations. So why did she subconsciously still think Grant was so fine? He'd dumped her!

GRANT WASN'T FINISHED GETTING ready before Sam left the trailer, taking his truck into town. His partner hadn't said two words to him about where he was going or what he was doing. All Grant knew was that he'd be at the Ugly Stick later that evening, hoping for a chance to see Mona.

Grant's lips curved upward. Thank goodness he'd gotten her to commit to dinner with him. At least he was one move ahead of his partner. Where Sam was starting from nothing, Grant had a history with Mona. Although not necessarily a good history with her. Other than when he'd called it off, they'd been very happy together and they never seemed able to get enough of each other.

Then again, Dalton had been part of that picture. He'd led off the ménage. Would Mona be satisfied with only one cowboy when she'd been accustomed to two?

Doubt assailed Grant as he drove into Temptation. Closing in on six o'clock he eased down Main Street, not wanting to be late, but not early either. He felt like he did on his first date in high school, expecting to be graded on every little thing he did. He deserved it after how he'd treated Mona. But it didn't make it easier knowing that.

He parked in the empty parking space in front of the Shear Safari Salon, checked that his hair wasn't standing on end and that his fly was zipped before he dropped down out of the truck. His hands were clammy and his pulse kicked up a notch.

Shit. He *knew* Mona. They weren't strangers. Then again, he didn't necessarily know the Mona who'd been dumped by a cowboy who'd promised to love her forever. He pushed his shoulders back. *Suck it up, dude.* He'd screwed up and now he was there to make it up to her.

Grant reached for the door handle to the salon, but the door was locked. He peered through the salon window into the dark interior. The lights were all turned off for the evening. Then he remembered her apartment was above the shop and the stairs were around the side.

He pivoted and rounded the corner of the building, stopping short.

In the alley between the buildings stood a white pickup truck with North Dakota tags.

Sam.

Anger sent Grant charging up the stairs. Before he reached the top, the door swung open and Mona stood in the doorframe and greeted him with a smile. "Oh, there you are. We were just about to come looking for you."

"We?"

"Sam beat you here." She hooked Sam's arm and brought him into the doorframe. "He said you insisted on him accompanying us to dinner," Mona said. "I think that was really magnanimous of you, seeing that Sam and I have…you know…done the nasty." Mona stepped out into the waning sunlight in a pale yellow dress that complemented her dark brown hair to perfection.

When she stepped out and turned to lock the door behind Sam, the sun shone through the fabric outlining every curve of her body beneath.

Grant's breath caught in his throat and he almost choked, coughing, sputtering and nearly falling back down the stairs.

Mona hurried down to stand on the step above the one he was on. "Are you okay?"

"You're wearing *that*?"

She smiled and pivoted on the step. "I know, it's

wicked, isn't it? All the old biddies will have their tongues wagging by the time we leave the restaurant."

Grant glanced around at the ground below them, wondering if anyone else could see through her dress like he could. "Maybe we should get our dinner to go and come back here to eat."

"I wouldn't dream of it. Two hulking cowboys would give me claustrophobia in my tiny apartment." She pushed past him and started down the stairs.

When Grant didn't follow, she glanced back at him. "Just so you know…" she raised the skirt on the back of her dress until he and Sam could see the rounded globe of her derriere, "…I'm not wearing panties." She pressed a finger to her lips. "Shh. Don't tell."

Then she skipped down the rest of the steps, her skirt flapping just enough to show a little ass.

Grant sucked in a huge breath and blew it out. "Holy hell."

"You're tellin' me." Sam patted Grant's back.

He shot a glare at the Lakotan. "This was supposed to be *my* date."

"Yeah, and I want my chance with her too. So we give her the menu and let her choose."

Grant growled. "I should give up team ropin' all together."

"What's that got to do with Mona?"

"*Everything.*" He stomped down the stairs to the bottom. "We'll take my truck."

"Actually, I thought we'd go in my car," Mona said. "Nick McBride got it fixed and delivered it just a few minutes ago. I want to try it out."

"Shotgun," Sam called out before Grant could think.

"I'm *not* crawling into the back."

"Suit yourself." Sam slid into the passenger seat and settled back with a wide smile.

Grant growled. This date was not going according to his plan. "I'll take my truck and meet you there."

"Good idea," Mona agreed brightly.

And that's how Grant ended up driving alone on his date with Mona, while his partner rode with her. His hands had etched permanent grooves in the steering wheel as he followed them to the restaurant. On the four short blocks from her shop, he imagined what Sam might be doing or saying as they sat in the close confines of her Camaro. Hell, she wasn't wearing panties! Sam could cop a whole lot of feel in four blocks.

His heart pounding against his ribs, Grant tailed Mona so close that if she'd jammed on her brakes, he'd have driven up her tailpipe.

Damn. So much for giving her a chance to get to know him again. He'd have to even the odds at the diner and maybe later that night when she got off work.

He still loved Mona, even after all these years and he'd do anything to win her back. As far as he was concerned, it was game-on with Sam. Let the better man win. *And let the better man be me.*

CHAPTER NINE

*A*fter the striptease with Bunny, Mona's sex drive was on hyper-alert. When Sam had shown up at her door, she'd wanted to pull him in as the most convenient male and hump his bones until that itch that had started with the stripper music was thoroughly scratched.

Bunny had dressed quickly, made excuses and skipped out on her, maybe sensing Mona wanted more than a handshake from the tall, dark Lakotan.

With Grant on his way and Sam already there, Mona had to change her mindset and fast. Sam knew about her and Grant's past. That was clear. And the fact he'd arrived earlier than Grant led Mona to think he'd wanted to be one step ahead, as if he was in competition to win her affections, just like Grant.

When she stopped to think about it, it felt good to be fought over. Especially after such a long dry spell. She'd damn well turned the tables in her favor. Thus the happy inclusion of the two men at dinner.

She plugged her smart phone into the dash and selected the song she'd been dancing to earlier, the music making her pussy throb. With one hand on the steering wheel, she moved her upper body to the sexy rhythm.

Sam leaned toward her. "Mona, I wanted to talk to you before we sit down to dinner with Grant."

"Sorry, Sam, I just have to listen to this song." She increased the volume, shutting out any chance at conversation with the man until they arrived at the diner. If all went well, she'd have both men so hot and bothered they'd be ready to do just about anything to get into her panties.

Oh, wait. I'm not wearing panties.

She had to give Bunny credit for that idea. Mona smiled, liking how naughty it felt and how hot it made her. After three long years, she was ready to set the town on fire. It was probably a good thing she had to work that night or she'd be in big trouble with these two men.

At least this way the anticipation would be heightened and she'd be more than ready to explore the possibilities with Sam and Grant. A shiver rippled across her senses, sending a rush of warmth to her center. *Oh yeah, let's get the party started.*

Inside the restaurant, Mona chose a narrow booth that barely had enough room between the table and the backs of the seats for the two hulking men to slide into.

Sam stuck to Mona like glue, easing into the booth beside her.

Grant's fists clenched and he looked like he wanted to punch Sam's lights out.

Mona hid her grin and waited for Grant to scoot across the opposite seat in front of her. She'd make sure he was glad he sat there.

"Hi, I'm Mandy." A pretty young woman wearing an old-fashioned apron, stopped at their table. "I'll be your waitress."

As soon as the server took their order for drinks, Mona slipped her right foot out of her sandal and stretched her leg toward Grant, glad this was the narrowest booth in the restaurant. "Tell me, boys, how was the team roping event today?"

As Grant opened his mouth to respond, her toes curved around the back of his calf. He jumped slightly before he realized what she was doing. His eyes narrowing quizzically, he responded, "We had the best time of the event today."

"Congratulations." Mona's hand rested on Sam's leg as she stared across at Grant. "I know you've told me before, but humor me. How does it work in team roping? Who ropes what?" Her fingers smoothed across the top of Sam's leg, working their way toward his crotch. At the same time, she raised her foot to the inside of Grant's thigh.

"Uh," Sam said, his face turning a ruddy red.

"I'm the header." Her toe slid along the inside of Grant's thigh and he sucked in a breath, finishing in a rush, "I rope the horns."

"And I'm the heeler." Sam gulped when her fingers found the hard ridge of his cock beneath his jeans. "I rope the steer's hind legs."

"I bet it takes some coordination and teamwork to get the animal all tied up like that. Sounds fascinating." Mona's toe touched Grant's crotch at the same time as her hand curled around Sam's. "You two must practically read each other's minds."

Sam stared across the table at Grant.

The two men sat in silence, their faces a warm shade of red beneath their tans.

Mandy reappeared with a tray of drinks and Mona sat up straight, retracting her hand and foot.

"Have y'all decided?" Mandy asked.

Mona had, and she was setting out to get just what she wanted, more sex and to teach a couple men some lessons. "I'll have the filet mignon, rare," she said, then added fast and low, "With a double side of horny cowboys."

Mandy's brow wrinkled. "I'm sorry, I didn't catch that last part. What did you say?"

Mona smiled. "Nothing."

Sam scrambled for his menu, opening it upside down, then closing it. "I'll have what she's having —the filet."

Grant didn't even try to look at the menu. He shifted in his seat, adjusting his jeans. "Make mine the same."

"Three filets, rare." Mandy made a note on her order pad then glanced up. "What sides would you like?"

"I don't care," Sam said, his voice a bit too sharp. "Use your imagination."

"Same," Grant bit out.

Mona took her time, loving that the men were already flustered by her attention and that they had to have heard her whispered comment. "What are the options?" she asked, knowing it would keep the waitress there longer, frustrating the men even more.

Mandy stared at the corner and recited the list.

The two men sat straight and stiff, probably in more ways than one, and Mona grinned. For once she felt like she was in the position to make things happen. She had the power over the men in her life. The feeling was heady. "I'll have the house salad with the vinaigrette on the side and a baked potato."

The waitress wrote down her order. "What would you like on your baked potato?"

Grant moaned and Sam's hand clenched around his napkin, dropping it over his lap.

A giggle threatened to bubble up and escape Mona's throat. She swallowed hard to keep it at bay and answered, "Bacon bits, cheese and sour cream."

"Gentlemen?" Mandy addressed them.

"Same," Sam and Grant said at once.

After Mandy left, Mona added in a sexy, sultry voice, "I love the creamy stuff on my potato, don't you? The way it gets all hot and wet and spreads across the milky white potato."

"Yeah." Sam tugged at his jeans.

"Sure," Grant said through clenched teeth.

"Will you both be at the Ugly Stick tonight?" Mona asked, her voice upbeat, innocent.

"I will," Sam jumped in. "I'd be happy to give you a lift there and back home."

"I can drive myself, now that my car is fixed. Besides, I'll be working a late-night private party." She laid a hand on his arm and smiled at the tall, dark, cowboy. "But thanks for coming to my rescue last night. I don't know how my night would have gone if you hadn't showed up."

"Anything for you, darlin'," Sam said.

Grant's face darkened. "Maybe I should leave the two of you alone?"

Mona laughed. "Don't be silly. I enjoy having *both* of you here."

"That's not exactly the idea," Grant muttered. "I thought we'd have a quiet dinner, just the two of us."

Mona's brows rose. "Maybe next time. Tonight, I'm privileged to have the company of two very handsome cowboys. And I like it."

Sam captured her hand. "And I'm happy to be having dinner with my partner and the prettiest girl in the state."

Grant coughed into his napkin, the sound coming out more like, "Bullshit."

"Did you say something?" Mona asked, putting Grant on the spot when she knew exactly what he'd said.

"No, ma'am."

Mona's eyes narrowed, but then she turned to Sam and smiled. "Did you know that my best friend, Bunny, has two men in her life?"

"Interesting," Sam said.

"I think so." Mona shifted his hand to her thigh. "They all live in the same house. Which I find…intriguing." She rested her elbow on the table, her chin propped in her hand. "Don't you?" Mona batted her long brown eyelashes, first at Sam and then at Grant.

Grant's face reddened. "It doesn't work."

"Bunny would disagree with you. And Libby, the bartender at the Ugly Stick, lives with two men. Isabella, one of the waitresses, lives with *three*." Mona crossed her arms. "You'll have a hard time convincing them it doesn't work, when it obviously does."

"It's not a lifestyle for everyone," Grant grumbled.

Mona nodded, her memories drifting back to when Dalton had introduced her to the concept, then had been such a pig and moved on. She could see where Grant was hesitant to engage in such a relationship again. Mona was equally hesitant, but open to the concept. She lifted her leg again and ran her toes along the inside of his thigh. "I'm just sayin' it's intriguing between the right people. What are your thoughts, Sam?"

Sam's brow furrowed. "I actually haven't known any people in that situation. I suppose it could work. If the parties involved are committed to the effort." His fingers slipped to the inside of her thigh, brushing against her center, the thin dress not much of a barrier to his rough hands.

Her pussy creamed at his light touch.

"My thought exactly." She shot a big smile at Grant, her breath hitching a bit. "It takes a great deal of trust." Her gaze leveled on Grant. "Don't you think?"

"Yeah. And love." He reached beneath the table and captured her foot, placing it at the center of his crotch. "It's not all about the sex. Though that can be satisfying. What are you gettin' at, Mona?"

She looked away, heat rising up her own neck and into her cheeks, her body aching for more than touching and feeling beneath the table. "I'm just making conversation," she said with a brightness that was beginning to feel strained.

Grant pressed her foot to the hardening swell beneath his jeans. "I don't think so."

Oh yeah, he was turned on, but then so was she and the restaurant seemed even smaller and more claustrophobic than usual.

"Your steaks." Mandy sailed to the rescue with a laden tray filled with plates of steaming food. "Just the way you ordered."

When Grant reached out to take a plate from the waitress, Mona snatched her foot away from his crotch, her toes tingling with awareness of just how much she was affecting him.

Trouble was, it was equally affecting her, killing her appetite for food while intensifying her hunger for—her lower belly clenched—sex.

She sank into silence, toying with her food, as the men dug into their steaks. When they'd cleared their plates, she asked Mandy for a box to take hers home.

"I need to get back to my apartment and change into my work clothes."

Sam jumped up. "Grant, get the check, I'll see Mona home."

Mona raised a hand. "No, if you don't mind, I don't want to hurry you two. Grant can give you a ride back to your truck. If you're at the Ugly Stick later, I'll see you there."

Sam grabbed her hand. "I'll be there." He shot a glance at Grant. "When can I see you alone?"

"I don't know, Sam." Her head was in a whirl of passion and she had to get away from them to be able to think straight.

"She's going out with me next." Grant took her other hand.

Mona tugged her hand free. "Sorry, guys. I really have to go. And let me leave you with this." She stood two feet away from them, out of reach. "I'm not sure I'm ready for either one of you, alone. But I might consider both."

"Mona, wait." Grant reached out.

"Mona, please." Sam took a step toward her.

"No." Mona held up her hand. "I'm not going to be forced to choose between you two. I'm not even sure I want to be with either one of you. Frankly, I don't want to be hurt again and all I can see at this moment is a whole lot of heartache."

She turned and ran out of the restaurant. Hot, horny, confused and needing a good unbiased shoulder to cry on.

SAM STARTED to go after her, but Grant hooked his arm. "Let her go."

"Why? You did that three years ago, and this is what happened."

Grant nodded. "She doesn't trust either one of us."

"Thanks to you and Faulkner for walking out on her."

"If it makes you feel any better, she probably wouldn't trust any man at this time."

Sam's brows angled downward. "That's supposed to make me feel better?"

"No, but at least you know it's not just you." Grant tossed some bills on the table. "Come on."

"I'll walk."

"Suit yourself. I'll get to the salon before you either way."

"Like hell you will." Sam burst through the door and ran all the way down Main Street to Mona's place.

Grant passed him and parked in front of her shop.

Sam got there three minutes later, after Grant had already circled to the back.

His heart hammering and out of breath, Sam rounded the corner to the stairs.

"Don't bother, she's not letting either one of us in." Grant descended slowly, taking one step at a time.

"She and I had a beautiful night together...*without* you." Sam stomped to his truck. "Then you walk back into her life and screw her up, and my chances with her."

"You just met Mona."

"Doesn't matter. Have you ever heard of love at first sight?" Sam wasn't even sure that's what he was feeling, but he knew he liked being with Mona and wanted the opportunity to get to know her better.

"Did you ever think that maybe she's using you?" Grant said.

Sam stopped and spun toward Grant, fists raised. "Take that back."

Grant held up his hands. "Look, I'm not trying to start a fight. But think about it. You two have had one night together, not a lifetime."

"You left her alone for three years."

"I know and I've regretted every minute of it. You also know what I was like when we met. A complete, fucked-up mess. I had to get my act together before I could come back here."

"Your point?" Sam unclenched his fists and crossed his arms.

"She could be scared of a relationship with either one of us." Grant dug his hands into his pockets. "She said it herself that she doesn't want to be hurt again."

"And what's this got to do with her using me?"

"As a shield. Me too, for that matter. If she has both of us in the picture, she doesn't have to choose. She can use me to shield her heart from you and vice versa."

Sam shook his head. "Sounds like psycho-bullshit to me."

"Yeah, but she didn't want to be alone with either one of us tonight."

"She was alone with me last night."

"True. And she might like you enough to feel threatened."

"I'd never hurt her."

"I know that, and you know that, but she might not believe it."

Sam leaned back against his truck and raked a hand through his hair. "What do we do?"

"Give her what she wants."

Before Grant finished talking, Sam was shaking his head. "You're my friend, and I share a trailer with you, but damned if I'm gettin' naked with you to win over Mona. She has to choose between me and you."

Grant shrugged. "I guess you aren't as serious about winning her over as you think you are."

"I am, but I'll do it on my terms."

"Good luck with that." Grant turned toward his truck. "Let me know when you're ready to work as a team." He left Sam standing by his truck and drove away.

His head whirling with what Mona had said, what Grant had reinforced and his own preferences, Sam glanced up at Mona's door. Was she worth the trouble?

His groin tightened at the image of her lying naked beside him in bed, her dark hair spilled out over the pillow, her smile and the way she laughed.

Damn. He was too close to believing what he'd said to Grant about love at first sight. Torn between climbing the stairs to demand Mona make a choice, and leaving and never looking back, Sam stood for a long time, straddling the fence, half-hoping Mona would come out of her apartment and tell him she'd been pulling his leg about demanding a threesome or nothing.

After ten minutes, he finally gave up, climbed into

his truck and headed for his trailer. He'd sit this one out. No way in hell he was going to crawl in bed with Mona and his partner. It wasn't right.

The image of the three of them lying naked in bed grew in his mind and his body tightened, his cock swelling. *Holy hell.* Now he was lusting after something that would never happen. Not in a million years.

CHAPTER TEN

"Where's Audrey?" Mona asked Libby as soon as she entered the Ugly Stick Saloon.

Libby nodded toward the door to the back. "In the storeroom."

Without stopping to catch her breath, Mona burst through the door.

Audrey was with her fiancé, Jackson Gray Wolf, her jean skirt hiked up to her waist, her legs wrapped around Jackson and her hands braced on a beam behind her. With her head tilted back, she had her eyes squeezed shut. "Come on, Jackson. Fuck me like there's no tomorrow."

"Workin' it, babe." Jackson's jeans hung loose around his waist and he held her hips, his cock pumping into her like a jackhammer. "Make some noise."

She moaned and rocked her hips. "Come on, stud. Use that cock like you mean it. Make my pussy hot."

"Oh." Mona ground to a stop, her hand on the doorknob, her heart lodging in her throat.

Audrey's eyes opened and she tapped Jackson's shoulder. "Honey, we have company."

"She'll have to wait her turn," he gritted out without breaking his rhythm, thrusting into her, his body tensing. "Are you with me?"

Audrey raised one finger. "Just a minute, Mona." Then she was all attention on Jackson again.

"I can come back when you're not so...busy," Mona whispered.

"No, stay. It makes me hotter." Audrey's head tipped back again. "Flick my clit, honey. One more time and I'll blow."

He reached between them and stroked her where she wanted.

Audrey's back arched against the pole and she cried out. "Oh, yes! There. I'm coming."

"I'm with you, babe." Jackson thrust one last time and held her still, buried deep inside.

Mona stood with her mouth open. She'd heard from others who worked at the Ugly Stick that Audrey and Jackson had numerous sessions in the storeroom or the costume room behind the stage, often interrupted by one of her staff. This was a first time for Mona to walk in on the pair.

She'd never watched another couple making love. Audrey was right. It was damned hot and made Mona's insides even more inflamed than when she'd left Sam and Grant at the restaurant. Without realizing it, one hand rose to press against her tingling breasts and the other cupped her denim-covered crotch. Her core ached for release and her pussy creamed as the couple disengaged.

Jackson withdrew, letting Audrey's feet drop to the ground.

She handed him a towel, he mopped up his come and zipped his jeans before facing Mona. He winked. "Thanks. Couldn't have done it without you."

Audrey slapped his arm. "Liar. But yes, it was nice to have an audience." Audrey slipped her skirt down over her hips.

Mona was a little shocked and turned on by the fact the owner of the saloon wasn't wearing panties beneath her skirt.

"I'm just leaving." Jackson pressed a kiss to Audrey's lips and ducked out of the storeroom.

"Mona, I'm so glad you could help out tonight." Audrey hugged her as soon as the door closed behind Jackson.

Mona held on longer than normal, her body burning, tears welling in her eyes blurring her vision. "Holy crap, Audrey."

"I know." Audrey giggled. "Jackson's so damned hot I can't keep my hands off him." She pushed Mona to arm's length and brushed her hair from her eyes. "What's wrong, honey? You look tense and ready to cry."

"Oh, Audrey." A single tear slipped down Mona's cheek. "I don't know what to do."

Her boss tipped her chin up. "Oh, baby, are you in trouble with the law?"

Mona shook her head. "No."

"Oh dear. Are you pregnant?"

A laugh bubbled up Mona's throat. "No…no, I'm not." Although the thought of being pregnant made her even more confused and kind of sad.

Audrey shook her head. "If you're not in trouble with the law and you're not pregnant, everything else is easily handled. Spill it. What's got your panties in a twist? Or should I say *who*?"

"Grant and Sam," Mona said in a rush. "I don't know what to do about them."

"Honey, is that all?"

"Is that all? After three years of being celibate, I have two men wanting to take me out."

"I'm sorry, I'm not seeing the problem here." She rested her hands on her hips. "Sounds to me like you should be celebrating, not crying buckets of tears."

"I should, but I don't know who to choose."

"Do you love them both?" Audrey asked.

"I loved Grant three years ago."

"And now?"

"Hell, I still love him, but I'm not sure I trust him."

"What about Sam?" Audrey gave her a direct stare. "Did you know him before last night?"

"No."

"Have you even known him for twenty-four hours?"

"Almost." Mona knew how bad that sounded. "But we had sex last night."

"And?" Audrey prompted.

"It was great." Tears welled in her eyes. "He was gentle, considerate, passionate and wonderful."

"Did he ignite your flame, make your toes curl, get your motor running?" Audrey asked. "Did he make you want to do it in the storeroom?" She winked.

"Yes, yes and yes."

"I hear a *but* coming."

"But Grant does too."

Audrey lifted her hands. "Then have them both."

"It's not that simple." Mona scuffed her leopard print heel on the sticky barroom floor. "I told them they had to be willing to work with me as a team."

Audrey threw back her head and laughed. "Good for you."

"What do you mean?"

"If they love you enough to win your heart, they'll do this."

"What if they decide they can't?" Mona paced the short distance to a stack of boxes containing whiskey. "What if they both back out?"

"Then your problem is solved and you move on to another man…or men."

"Audrey!" Mona flung her hands up. "I don't want to lose them."

"Honey, my momma told me never to borrow trouble." Audrey gave her a quick hug. "See what happens and go from there."

"I know. That's about all I can do." She wondered if she'd been stupid to demand they take her on as a team.

If she could have only one of them, which would she choose?

"In the meantime, work will help keep your mind off your troubles. I throw myself into the job when I'm worried. It helps."

"Yeah. Thank goodness we'll be busy tonight."

"You still on for the private party at midnight?"

"I am. I need the cash. I thought I had a month, but the bank called today and said the property owner has another offer. I only have two weeks to come up with the cash."

"My offer still stands."

"I'm close, Audrey. I think between tips tonight, the party and tomorrow's tips, I'll just about have enough."

"Don't lose the shop because of your pride. I don't want to have to drive all the way to Hole in the Wall for a haircut."

"Thanks, Audrey."

"Now get out there and smile."

"I don't feel much like smiling."

"Then fake it 'til you feel it." Audrey opened the storeroom door and sent Mona out into the crowded saloon.

She really hoped Sam and Grant wouldn't show up that night. Then again, if they didn't, did that mean they weren't going to play her game? That neither one of them was interested enough to play by her rules?

Holy crap. Had she given up both of them because she didn't want to choose? Or had she done it because she was afraid?

GRANT ARRIVED at the Ugly Stick Saloon after ten o'clock. The place was packed. Many contestants had finished their events and were ready to blow off the steam from a stressful few days of events. Some of them were celebrating victory, others drowning their bad luck in whiskey and bourbon.

He should have been celebrating with his team-roping partner. They'd placed first in their event, cause for major celebration. Instead he was there alone and he didn't know Sam's whereabouts. Probably somewhere in the crowded saloon.

For the first couple hours after Mona left, Grant told himself to let her go. Sam wasn't interested in making good her challenge. Without him, Grant didn't have a chance at getting near Mona. Or did he? He'd convinced himself she was running scared and afraid to commit to either man. Which meant he'd have to try harder to woo her, to win her over, by showing her patience and understanding. He couldn't expect her to trust him just because he said he was sorry. He had to earn back her trust.

An evening that had started out on a bad foot could only get better. Moping around the trailer wouldn't buy him anything. So here he was in a crowded saloon, hoping to catch a glimpse and maybe a dance with Mona.

His gaze skimmed over the heads of the cowboys lucky enough to have snatched a seat in the place. A flash of dark shiny hair and the sway of smoothly rounded hips encased in a short, denim skirt caught his attention.

There she was, smiling at the customers, flirting and filling her pockets with tips. Damn, she was so pretty and natural, she made Grant's groin ache. He'd have to wade through a sea of cowboys to get to her. Hugging the walls, he inched his way around the room until he made it to the bar. A cowboy got up, tossed down a twenty and left. Grant grabbed the stool and sat.

"What can I getcha, cowboy?" Libby asked. "Oh, hey. Grant, right?"

"Yeah. Sam Adams, if you have it."

"Coming up." She turned to pull a beer out of a cooler, popped off the top and set it in front of him. "Just in time for the show."

The band in the corner announced that they would take a fifteen-minute break. Audrey climbed onto the bar, a microphone in her hand. "Are you ready to party?" she yelled.

The room full of cowboys all answered as one, "Hell, yeah!"

"Come on, girls. Show these fine men how it's done."

Audrey reached down and grabbed Kendall's hand, hauling her up onto the counter. Two other waitresses joined them and Mona was helped up by two swarthy-skinned cowboys, as the music started. Each woman wore a straw cowboy hat, short denim skirts and cowboy boots.

"Thanks, Mark. Thanks, Luke," she called out to them, twisting and kicking her heels up in step with the others on the bar.

The men in the crowd clapped, whistled and shouted as the women danced.

At the end of the dance, Audrey raised her microphone and, like the night before, she announced that whichever cowboy caught a hat, that cowboy got to dance with the girls on the bar.

His pulse leaping, Grant stood, easing his way toward the end of the bar where Mona danced. So far, she hadn't given any indication she'd seen him. Good. If he laid low until she launched the hat, he had a chance. If she saw him, she might throw it the other way.

The music came to a stop and the ladies on the bar ripped their hats off their heads and threw them.

Grant sprang into the air, his eye on the ball…or hat, in this case. Out of the corner of his eyes, he could see Sam leap into the air as well. A dozen other hands reached for the same hat. Just when he thought he had his hand on the prize, Sam snatched it from the other side.

They dropped to their feet at the same time, neither letting go of the straw hat. Grant tugged hard, trying to dislodge it, Sam tugged equally hard and the hat ripped in two.

The two men stared at the hat, then turned to Mona, who stood on the bar, her arms crossed, shaking her head. "Really?"

"Sorry, Mona. I'll buy you a new hat." Grant reached up to help her down.

Sam stood beside him. "No, I tore it, I'll buy you a new hat."

As the disappointed cowboys moseyed back to their chairs, Grant and Sam hovered in front of the bar, each holding out their hands, waiting for Mona to choose which she'd let help her down.

Finally, she ignored both of them, sat on the bar and scooted off without their help. "Come on, I'll dance with Sam first, then Grant. No fighting."

She grabbed Sam's hand and dragged him toward the dance floor, her lips moving, her voice drowned by the loud music and even louder cowboys.

Sam shot a triumphant grin over his shoulder at Grant.

His fists clenched, Grant could only watch from the sidelines as Sam danced away with Mona.

"What's the matter?" Dalton stopped next to Grant and chuckled. "Your partner get your girl?"

"Shut up, Dalton."

Dalton smirked. "She's nothin' but a tease. Not worth fightin' over." He crossed his arms. "If it hadn't been for her, we'd still be a team."

"No, if it hadn't been for you, I'd have been with Mona for the last three years." Grant grabbed the front of Dalton's shirt and jerked him close. "You fucked it up. Not me, and not Mona."

Dalton peeled Grant's fingers loose from his shirt and smoothed out the wrinkles. "You're a fool, Raleigh. No woman is worth the amount of trouble *that* one has caused."

"Get out of my face." Grant clenched his fists, fighting the urge to slug the bullshit out of his ex-partner.

"Look what happened with your first wife. She didn't even stay married to you a whole year before she slept with me then ran off with another cowboy. Did she?"

Grant closed his eyes and counted to three, then opened them and said, "Get the hell out of my face."

"And if I don't, whatcha gonna do about it?" Dalton waved him forward. "Come on. Take a swing."

Mona and Sam stopped in front of them. "Grant, your turn."

Reluctant to leave a fight Dalton started, Grant hesitated.

"If you're not going to dance with her, I will." Sam started to lead Mona back among the dancers.

"We'll dance," Grant said, his words tight. "Dalton's not worth it."

Sam placed Mona in his arms and gave them a shove toward the other dancers. "Go on then. I got this."

Before he left Dalton, Grant said, "Stay out of my life and leave Mona alone. She deserves better than you." Then he gathered Mona close and took off. When they rounded the end of the dance floor and headed back in Dalton's direction, Sam wasn't next to him.

"Leave it, Grant," Mona said. "Dalton's an ass. Sam didn't rise to his bait. Neither should you."

Grant settled into the steps, his gaze resting on her. "Mona, I meant it when I said I was sorry for leaving you."

"I know."

"What's it going to take to win you back?"

She stiffened in his arms, her steps slowing. "I told you."

"Sam's not into threesomes."

"Frankly, Grant, I don't want to talk about it. Let's get through this dance and you can go home."

"I'm not giving up."

"Why? To prove a point?" She stopped in the middle of the dance floor. "Did you ever really love me?"

"Yes. I loved you and still do." Other couples nearly bumped into them. "I'm not leaving now, because you're worth fighting for."

She stared up at him, her eyes swimming in unshed tears. "You didn't think so the last chance you had."

"Other things came up. I wasn't free to come back."

"Yeah, you married another woman." A tear slipped down her face. "How was I supposed to take that? You said you loved me. Then you turned around and married another woman. I guess I should at least be happy you ended it with a phone call. I was stupid and in love."

"I married Desiree because she was pregnant." There it was out. He'd told her. "Not because I loved her."

Mona stepped out of his arms. "She was pregnant when we were going out?"

"I didn't know it then."

"But you slept with her and then moved on to the next rodeo and slept with me." She dropped her arms to her sides. "How do I know you won't do it again? New town, new fuck-buddy."

He gripped her arms, his fingers digging into her soft flesh. "Because I love you. I don't want another woman in my life. There hasn't been one since you."

"Well, I don't want just you. If I can't have both you and Sam, I don't want either of you." The music ended on her last word. Mona walked off the dance floor and disappeared through a door into the back of the saloon.

Grant retraced his steps to the bar and ordered another whiskey, determined to take the edge off his anger and disappointment by blurring it with booze.

"You gonna let her walk away?" Sam appeared next to him.

"She made her wishes clear. It's both of us or neither."

"Let's go." Sam wove his way through the throng of rowdy cowboys.

Grant left his whiskey and followed. "Where are we going?"

"After Mona. Where else?" Sam turned toward the door leading to the back of the saloon where Mona had gone.

A large figure stepped in front of them.

Grant couldn't quite tell if the person was male or female.

"Employees only allowed in the back," she said in a low voice.

"We need to see Mona," Grant said.

"You and every other horny cowboy." She jerked her thumb. "Beat it."

"But—"

"You heard me."

"Greta Sue, let them through." The pretty straw-berry-blonde bar owner touched the massive woman's arm. "Mona knows them, and I approve." Her arm shot out to grab Grant's. "As long as they don't hurt her anymore." She leveled a sharp stare at Grant. "Got it?"

"Yes, ma'am." Grant nodded. "I never wanted to hurt her."

"Well, you did. She's backstage in the costume room. Now get in there and fix it."

Again, he replied, "Yes, ma'am."

Greta Sue stepped aside, allowing Grant and Sam to pass, then closed the gap with her big frame behind them.

As they entered the backstage area, Grant leaned toward Sam and whispered, "I take it you're in?"

Sam nodded. "I'm not excited by it. But I'm in. Whatever happens, don't be touchin' my dick."

"Goes both ways."

Sam stuck out his hand. "Deal."

They rounded a corner into the costume room and found Mona with her back to them, slipping out of her skirt and panties. She lifted the hem of her tank top and dragged it up over her head, her dark-brown hair falling down around her shoulders.

Both men ground to a stop and stared, speechless.

Grant's cock twitched and a knot the size of a walnut lodged next to his vocal chords. *God, she's beautiful.*

Still with her back to them, she reached back and lifted her hair up and let it sift through her fingers. Then she glanced over her shoulder, giving them the benefit of glimpsing one full, rounded breast. "Are you two going to stand there gawking or did you have a purpose for coming back here?"

Sam spoke first. "I'm in." He coughed and attempted to start again.

Grant touched his arm. "What he means is that we're here to give you what you want."

She reached into the rack of costumes and pulled out a red, sequined vest and held it to her front as she turned to face them. It barely covered her breasts and the triangle of hair at the apex of her thighs. One peaked nipple was visible, teasing them with its taut areola. "Do you really know what I want?"

"We think we do," Sam said. "You want both of us."

"To do what?"

Grant crossed to where she stood. "You want both of us to make love to you. To show you how much we care by working together to make you happy. Sam and I have an understanding and are willing to work as a team. Aren't we, Sam?" he said without looking back at his partner.

"We do and we are."

Grant's gaze never left Mona's, even as she glanced to Sam and back. He held out his hand. "Are you willing to give us the chance to prove ourselves?" What he wanted to say was, would she give him the chance to prove he cared enough to do anything to make her happy.

Her eyes widened and her breath escaped on a soft gasp. The hand holding the vest shook.

Grant inhaled the scent of her, honeysuckle and citrus, a poignant combination he had never forgotten. Her naked body within reach, made his tighten and ache.

Finally, she nodded. "Okay." Her hand dropped, the

hanger with the vest on it falling to the floor, exposing her entire body to Grant and Sam's perusal.

Grant reached out and touched her face.

Sam stepped up beside them. "How's this work? I've never been in a threesome."

"Kinda like team ropin'," Grant said with a grin. "I'll take the front, you get the back."

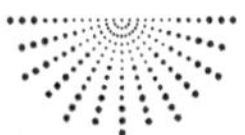

CHAPTER ELEVEN

Mona giggled nervously and leaned into Sam as he moved into position. "Umm."

Grant lifted her chin and claimed her lips in a kiss that left her breathless. He stroked her tongue while Sam's fingers settled on her waist and slid upward to cup her breasts, weighing the mounds in his big, rough hands.

Mona groaned into Grant's mouth and she reached for the buttons on his shirt, releasing them as quickly as she could.

She tingled all over and her blood burned through her system, igniting a desire so palpable, she ached with it. Mona had to be closer. Skin-to-skin wouldn't be enough to satisfy her hunger. With a desperate tug, she yanked Grant's shirt from his waistband and went to work on the top button of his jeans.

Sam tweaked the tips of her nipples, rolling the nubs between his thumbs and forefingers.

"Let me at one of those." Grant pushed aside one of Sam's hands and sucked the nipple between his lips, pulling hard.

Mona arched her back, urging him to take more into his mouth.

Sam's hand slid down her belly to the juncture of her thighs, threading through the curls.

"Oh, yes," Mona said, widening her stance, making it easier for him to part her folds and stroke the sensitive strip of flesh between. "There." She fumbled with the tab on Grant's jeans and pulled it down, releasing his stiff, thick cock into her palm, hard as steel and as soft as velvet, the mushroom head rounded and smooth. She licked her lips, anxious to taste him, wanting to take him into her mouth as she'd done before. Her channel washed with fresh juices, preparing her for what would come next. Anxious to get the party started, she turned to Sam and made quick work of his shirt, tossing it onto a stack of boxes. Her fingers slipped beneath his waistband and flicked the button loose.

Sam's hands closed over hers. "I don't know about this."

"You can keep your pants on, just let him out to play, like Grant." Mona unzipped his jeans and eased his cock free.

"Aren't you afraid someone will step back here and see us?" Sam asked.

"The fear of getting caught is half the excitement," Grant commented. He stepped away, grabbed a cape from the costumes, whipped it around with a flare and spread it across the floor. Then he dropped to his knees and tugged Mona down with him.

Still facing Sam, she knelt, her other hand taking his, guiding him to a kneeling position.

"This is weird," Sam remarked, his forehead furrowed.

Mona almost laughed. "Only for a moment." She dropped to all fours and took his cock in her hand, guiding it to her lips. "The weird ends here." With the tip of her tongue, she traced his bulbous head, lapping at the glistening come easing out of the tiny hole.

Sam's chest rose, his fingers reaching out to feather through her hair, pulling her closer.

She opened her mouth and sucked his cock in.

Sam's hips jerked, thrusting his dick in until it bumped against the back of her throat.

Grant lay down on his back and slid beneath Mona, aligning his head with her pussy. Then he ran his fingers along the insides of her thighs. "Lower, sweetheart."

Her insides on fire, Mona widened her knees so that she eased down over him until her clit was closer to his face, her body remembering the magic of his tongue, the way he made her scream for more.

He parted her folds and leaned up to flick her clit.

Mona moaned, her mouth closing tighter around Sam's dick.

Sam pulled out and slid back in as Grant flicked her again.

The intensity of sensations racing through her body

made her fingers curl in the cape and she sank lower on her knees.

Grant dipped his tongue into her channel, then back out, laving the nubbin packed with nerves, his attack spot on, sending her shooting to the edge with each stroke. He didn't let up, or back off.

Tingling began at her center, spreading outward to the very tips of her toes. A long slow groan rose up her throat and came out her mouth as a muffled scream around Sam's cock.

Just as Mona flew over the edge, Grant scooted out from under her. His hands curled around her hips and he positioned himself behind her, between her legs.

"Protection?" Sam gritted out.

Leaning over to reach for his jeans, Grant unearthed his wallet and pulled a foil packet from inside. He tore it open and slid the condom over his cock, then positioned it at Mona's entrance.

Her pussy creamed, her ass clenched and she waited for him to penetrate.

He touched her there with the tip of his cock, hesitated, then replaced his dick with his fingers, soaking them in the liquid, dragging it up to her clit. Mona rocked back against his hand in rhythm with Sam's thrusts into her mouth.

Tension built again, and her belly tightened, her core aching for Grant to bury himself deep inside her.

He slid his thumb into her pussy, drenched it in her juices and then circled her anus.

Mona inhaled sharply as he thrust his thumb into the tight hole at the same time as he flicked the nubbin of nerves between her folds. Sensations bolted through her. Just as she teetered on the edge, Grant stopped flicking her and aligned himself behind her, then thrust into her channel, his cock sliding in easily. Her muscles clenched around him as he pulled out, creating suction to bring him back in.

He gripped her hips and pumped in and out of her, matching Sam's thrusts with his own.

Mona rocketed to orgasm at the same time Sam's fingers knotted in her hair and he pulled out of her mouth.

Grant thrust one last time and held her firmly against his groin as he came, cock twitching inside with the force of his release.

Mona dropped her face to the cape, ass in the air, moaning, her body wracked with spasms. Holy hell, he was every bit as good as she remembered. *Damn him.*

When the earth stopped shaking, Grant pulled free and eased her to her belly on the cape and then rolled her to her side. Grant lay down in front of her and caressed her breasts.

Sam lay down behind her and rested a hand on her hip, slowly rubbing a circle.

"I've missed you." Grant stroked the hair out of her face and tucked it behind her ear.

As she caught her breath, Mona stared into Grant's eyes, wanting to believe him. Wanting him to say he loved her and that he'd stay with her forever. More afraid than ever to let her heart be broken again.

Sam's hand rested on her hip without moving, his cock still hard, pressing into her buttocks.

He was a good man. Sam would never hurt her. Mona felt it deep inside. He was strong, considerate, sweet and his lovemaking was great. But he didn't stir her to the depths Grant did. "I've missed you too," she whispered.

With time, they could make a threesome work. Time she'd need to get to know Sam better. But did she want to? Was her heart open to loving two men? She liked the way his hand felt on her hip. And having Sam there would divide her love so that she didn't invest all of it in Grant, only to be disappointed when he left again.

Her head spun with different scenarios, all of which involved Grant leaving. She wasn't ready to trust him with her heart. And she didn't know Sam enough to commit to him. "I have to get to work." She jumped up and grabbed the fallen vest.

"Will you see us tomorrow?" Grant asked.

"I don't know." Mona shoved her hands into the sleeves of the vest and pulled it over her breasts, buttoning the front.

Sam tucked his hard cock inside his jeans, his mouth pressed into a thin line. "We're only here one more day. We need to know if we have someone to come back to."

Grant grabbed her hand and pulled it to his lips. "Say you want me...us. And I swear on my favorite horse, I'll be back as soon as the rodeo circuit is over."

She shook her head, grabbed a G-string from inside a backpack and slipped it up over her hips. "I don't know what I want. I'm confused." She stood in her thong and the vest, her eyes filling with tears. "I'm afraid."

Sam touched Grant's arm. "Let her think on it." He nodded to Mona. "We'll find you tomorrow. Sleep on what we've said. Maybe you'll feel better about it in the morning."

She nodded, a tear sliding down her face. "Thank you."

Hooking Grant's arm, he dragged him out of the costume room as two other women passed them, going in.

A redhead smiled and winked at Sam. "Stick around, sweetie, the party starts at midnight."

As soon as they disappeared out of sight, Mona sat on a stack of boxes and buried her head in her hands. What was she going to do? She loved Grant as much, if not more than when they'd first met. Was it enough to sustain a relationship with a man who'd be on the road half the year?

And what about Sam? She'd pushed him into a threesome he obviously hadn't felt comfortable with. But he'd agreed to it, though he'd seemed awkward and a little uncomfortable with another man in the room. He hadn't even come. Now that he'd engaged in a ménage with her, did she owe him her love ever after? She barely knew him, but what she did know was that he would be loving and caring. She feared she'd used him to keep some distance between her and Grant.

For three years, she'd promised to never fall in love with another rodeo cowboy. They had a history of love-'em-and-leave-'em that had bitten her before.

But if she let Grant walk out this time, he may never

come back. Did she want to let him go? Would fear stand in her way of possibly having the love of her life?

"Mona, honey?" Charli Sutton rested a hand on her shoulder. "Are you okay?"

Mona shook her head. "No. I'm not okay."

"You don't have to dance tonight. The crowd will be just as happy with two girls as three."

"No. I need the money, or I'll lose my business."

"Hear that, Kendall?" Charli said. "We need to dance extra sexy tonight. We need to rake in the tips."

"Mona, you can have my share of the tips," Kendall said. "I'd planned on using the money to buy Ed a new barbeque grill. But if it's between keeping my favorite hairdresser and a grill, the money's yours."

"Mine too, for that matter," Charli added. "Can't have you going out of business. You're the only one who knows how to cut my hair."

Mona wiped away the tears and smiled at her friends. "No, really. I'll be fine. I've got just about enough to make the down payment for the loan. Tonight and tomorrow night will round it off and I'll be good." With a sigh, she pushed to her feet and hugged Charli and Kendall. "But thanks." The women at the Ugly Stick Saloon pulled together when someone needed help. It was a legacy Audrey had started and continued to perpetuate.

She wished they could help her decide what to do about Grant and Sam, but she figured she'd have to make that choice on her own. She'd have no one else to blame if her world came crashing down around her.

"GRANT, I'VE BEEN THINKIN'." Sam sat across the table from his partner at PJ's Diner the following morning.

"Oh, yeah?" Grant said, the first two words for the day, his hands wrapped around a coffee mug like it was a life preserver.

"Yeah." Sam leaned forward. "I've come to the conclusion that you and Mona belong together."

"Wish she'd come to that conclusion." He tipped his mug and drank, then set it back on the table. "I'd about decided she'd rather be with you."

"Seriously. The only way you're going to convince her is to show her how serious you are about the relationship."

"I thought that's what I did last night. I let you be a part of making love with her."

"Like you said, I think she's using me."

"She's not that mean-spirited."

"I know that," Sam said. "But I don't think she realizes she's using me against you."

"How so?"

"She's afraid to love you again. Apparently you hurt her really bad last time you came to town." Sam's gut twisted. He'd grown fond of Mona himself, and the thought of anyone hurting her didn't sit well with him. "You screwed up so royally you've got to do something big to show her you mean to stay this time."

Grant turned his mug around and turned it again. "And if I do something really big and she still refuses to believe me, then what?"

"You walk away." Sam shrugged. "I'm not an expert on love. All I know is that if you leave without trying, you'll regret it the rest of your life." He stared hard at his friend. "And frankly, I don't want to be the one to have to pull your ass out of the bottom of a whiskey bottle."

Raising his hand, Grant said, "I'm not going there again. I promised."

"Yeah, and you haven't been turned down by Mona yet. And hopefully you won't be. But you gotta come up with something that will absolutely convince her you mean to be with her for the long haul."

Across the table, Grant sat for several long moments in silence. "I don't deserve you as a friend."

"No, you don't." Sam smiled. "But I'm stuck with you."

"I should have been upfront with you. I knew you liked her and wanted to get to know her better. But seeing you two together nearly killed me."

"You could have said something in the very beginning."

"I know." Grant stared down at his coffee. "All I can say in my defense is that I've loved her for a long time, and I know, without a doubt, she's the one for me."

"Then don't screw up this time." Sam glared at him, then his brows eased up. "I haven't known her that long. You have. I guess I'll get over it. All your talk of buying a ranch kinda got to me."

Grant nodded. "Yeah, and the rodeo has a way of making a man old before his time."

"But I'm not as old as you are. Guess I can wait a little longer before I settle down." Sam grinned. "I think I've always known Mona's heart was somewhere else.

Never thought it would be with my no 'count partner." He stuck out his hand. "No hard feelin's."

"None here." Grant gripped Sam's hand and shook it. Then he slapped his palm on the table. "I know what I have to do, and I've been wanting to do it anyway for a long time."

"Tell me."

"It involves you gettin' a new team ropin' partner."

"You're not goin' back to Dalton, are you?"

"No way in hell." Grant pushed to his feet. "Think you can convince Mona to come to the rodeo just before I do the saddle bronc ridin'?"

"I'll do my best. If I have to hogtie and kidnap her, she'll be there."

"Good. I have to go get ready. I ride around one in the afternoon. Wave a red bandana or something so I can pick you out of the crowd. I need to know if she came."

"Will do." Sam stood and clapped his hand on his partner's back. "Good luck."

"Thanks." Grant hugged Sam. "I'll need it."

Grant practically ran out the door.

Sam sat back in the booth, thinking through what he had to do in order to get Mona to the rodeo on time.

"I hear you might be lookin' for a new team ropin' partner." The woman Grant had left the bar with two nights before slipped into the seat across from him and stuck her hand out. "Tacey Reese."

"Sam—"

"Whitefeather," she finished. "I know."

"I'm not lookin' for a new partner."

"Givin' up rodeoing?"

"Nah. Just not lookin' yet."

"If you change your mind, I'm pretty good. All you gotta do is give me a shot. I'll prove it to you."

Sam glanced across the table. "You got a lot of balls asking before we've officially announced anything."

"Had a long conversation with Grant the other night."

"Was that all you had with him?" Sam glared at Tacey, his loyalties still with Mona.

She raised her hands. "Let me tell you, I tried to have a lot more. He wasn't buying it."

Sam nodded slowly. "Been a crazy couple of days in Temptation."

"You're tellin' me." She leaned forward, her elbows on the table, her long sandy-blonde hair swinging down around her shoulders, her gray eyes shining. "So what are you going to do to get Mona to the rodeo?"

"Not sure yet."

"She has to have some friends who'd help run interference. You need to contact them first and get them on board."

"Good idea." Sam smiled. "So what's your story? Why help someone you don't even know?"

"I might look like a tomboy and ride as well as any man, but deep down, I'm just a silly romantic." She shrugged. "So sue me."

"If all goes as planned, I'll be at loose ends tonight. You have plans?"

"Depends on what you have in mind? If it's shoveling horse shit, I get enough of that with my own horse."

"Feel like dancing at the Ugly Stick?"

"Can I lead?"

Sam laughed. "You bet."

"Then let's get your plan rollin'." She rose and held out her hand. "I have a new dress to buy before tonight."

Mona yawned and turned the sign in the front of her shop to Open. She hadn't slept a wink the night before. Today was the last day Grant would be performing in the rodeo. He had no need to stay for the last day once his event was over. He'd pack up his trailer, and he and Sam would move on to the next town.

Her heart heavy and no nearer to making a decision, Mona grabbed her broom and swept the clean floor.

The bell over the door rang announcing Bunny's entrance. "I'm going to have to buy you a new broom by the end of the day if you keep that up."

"I have to sweep."

"Man troubles still? I heard you, Grant and Sam had the costume room to yourselves for a while at the Ugly Stick last night."

Her cheeks heating, Mona swept harder. "Gossip spreads like wildfire around here."

Bunny hugged her, forcing her to stop. "I think it's great. Two men can be wonderful."

"If you're in love with both of them."

"And you aren't?" Bunny stood out of the way of the swishing broom.

"Yes...no... Oh, I don't know." The broom moved faster.

"Honey, you have to figure it out."

"I know!" Mona stopped sweeping, rolled her shoulders and went back to it. "I just don't know if I can put my heart out there again. What if Grant leaves again and doesn't come back for three more years?"

"Grant, huh? What about Sam?" Bunny sat at the appointment counter, trailing her hand over the appointment book. "Is he an option?"

"I thought he was, but now I don't know."

Bunny jumped up. "Well, honey, you better decide soon. I'm sure those men aren't going to wait around for you forever." She hurried toward the door. "Sorry, I just remembered, I have to get some orders out. See you later."

Mona stopped sweeping to stare at the door. Bunny usually stuck around, listened and offered advice when Mona was troubled. And she really needed some help right then.

With no one to talk out her problems with, Mona swept, hoping it would clear away the fog of indecision.

The phone rang. Mona answered and it was Mrs. Smith, her noon appointment, calling to reschedule. Her dog was sick and she had to take it to the vet.

A few minutes later, Jodi Hughes called to

reschedule her one o'clock, claiming she couldn't get off work because someone else had called in sick.

Two reschedules in one day wasn't unheard of, but when the third and fourth customer called to reschedule the two and three o'clock hours, Mona wondered if the rest of Temptation had heard of her indiscretion in the back of the Ugly Stick and they were boycotting her business. Unfortunately, she had been counting on that money to help pay the bills and put toward the down payment she needed in two weeks.

She was in the shampoo room at the back of the shop, sweeping corners she'd missed the night before, when the bell over the front door jangled.

"I'll be right with you, Mrs. Biedel," she called out. At least her nine-thirty hadn't called to reschedule.

"It's not Mrs. Biedel, it's me, Joseph Spillman."

"Oh." Mona had counted all her tips and the money she'd squirreled away over the past few weeks and was a little less than one hundred dollars short.

She rounded the corner and stopped.

Mr. Spillman had a pained expression on his face. "The shop owner had a death in the family and the property needs to be moved. I asked him for another two weeks, but I'm afraid he's ready to take the offer from the other buyer today, if you're not ready to commit."

Commitment had been her problem all along with Grant. When she was ready to commit, he wasn't. Now he was ready and she was waffling. The shop had been another commitment dilemma as well. When the past shop owner had asked if she wanted to buy it, she'd waffled, not certain she was ready for the responsibility. Now that she was, she was short almost a hundred dollars. A measly hundred dollars.

"I'd planned on stopping by to see you tomorrow. I'll have the money for you then."

"I need it today."

Mona's heart plummeted. "They won't wait one day?"

"I'm sorry, Miss Daley."

"If you could wait for a moment, I'll run and get my money." *At least what I have. Oh God. Oh God.* It wasn't going to be enough.

Mona left Mr. Spillman in the shop and ran up the back steps to her apartment, her stomach sick at the thought of losing the building she'd put so much work into to make it the pretty little beauty shop it was. She pulled out the rooster cookie jar where she'd kept the money she'd been saving. With the ceramic rooster in her hands, she ran back down the steps to the shop.

Her pulse slamming through her veins and out of breath, she turned the jar over and emptied it on the counter, praying she'd miscounted and there'd be an extra ninety-eight dollars and twenty-five cents among the bills and change.

As Mr. Spillman started counting, Bunny entered, the bell over the door ringing loudly in the silence. Her questioning gaze met Mona's and she pointed at the man's back.

Mona nodded. "My time's up," she said quietly.

"How much more do you need?" Bunny asked.

"This cash, plus what I have in my savings account

will leave me about a hundred short."

Bunny turned to leave. "I'll get my checkbook."

"*No.* You have bills to pay." Mona shook her head. "I can't let you."

"You'll pay me back. I know you're good for it."

"I can't let you. Borrowing money from friends strains a relationship, and I can't afford to lose you now." She touched Bunny's shoulder. "But thanks for offering."

"Fine. Be that way." Bunny left the salon, letting the door slam behind her.

Mona's chest squeezed. Had she offended Bunny and strained her relationship by refusing the money? A hundred dollars. She might make that in tips that night and pay Bunny back in less than twenty-four hours. Was she piling one mistake on top of another?

Mr. Spillman continued counting.

Mona didn't feel a bit sorry for him having to go through the nine hundred dollars of ones, fives, tens and quarters, dimes, nickels and pennies. She'd worked hard for every bill and coin.

Five minutes into the count, Charli entered the shop, Kendall in tow. "We just stopped by to let you know that Audrey counted the tips wrong last night. She shorted you forty dollars." Charli handed her a wad of wrinkled cash.

Mona eyed the money without taking it. "Bunny said something to you, didn't she?"

"I don't know what you're talking about." Kendall tossed the cash onto the pile Mr. Spillman was still counting. "Audrey asked us to bring it by this morning.

She'd have delivered it herself, but she's on a liquor run to Dallas with Jackson. Seems the cowboys are drinking more this year than last. Should be a good year for the Ugly Stick."

The bell over the door rang again and Libby burst in. "I found this twenty under a beer bottle last night at one of your tables after you left."

Mona laughed. "And you just happened to stop by to leave it with me?"

"I was on my way to…" Libby glanced left then right, her gaze shooting to the door, "…the drugstore for condoms. You know the guys—always in the mood." She winked and skipped out the door, the color high in her cheeks.

Bunny entered, waving a twenty. "Remember the time you loaned me twenty dollars to buy groceries when I was flat broke and going through my divorce?"

Mona shook her head. "You paid me back."

"No, I didn't." She smiled brightly and tossed the bill on the stack of money. "But I have now."

"I'm not taking your money," Mona said.

Charli, Kendall and Bunny each planted their hands on their hips and tipped back their chins.

Bunny spoke for all three. "It's not *our* money. It's *your* money and… Yes. You. Are."

Mr. Spillman looked up from his pocket calculator and announced. "With the money you have in your savings account at the bank, plus what you have here, you're still eighteen dollars and twenty-five cents short." He glanced at the women in the room, sighed and dug his wallet out of his pocket and added a twenty to the cash. "My wife would kill me if this shop closed because I was too stingy to pitch in." He stuck out his hand. "Congratulations, the bank will approve the loan for you."

Mona took his hand and pulled him into a hug, her heart turning somersaults.

Rattled by the embrace, Mr. Spillman gathered up the cash and, promising to deposit it to her account and cut a check to the real estate agent, he left the shop.

Mona squealed and hauled the women into her arms, tears slipping down her cheeks. "I'm going to own my own building! All because of you."

Bunny shook her head. "You did it yourself."

"We're so happy for you," Charli said.

"And we get to keep the best beautician this town has ever had." Kendall laughed and danced around.

Amid smiles and well-wishes, Kendall and Charli left soon after.

Bunny grasped her hand one final time. "I'd stay and chat, but we both have work to do."

Mrs. Biedel entered the shop and Mona got started on her morning customers, finishing up all her appointments at ten minutes before eleven. Her heart was lighter and her thoughts turned to Grant and Sam more times than she cared to admit. With her entire afternoon free, she decided to close the shop and go somewhere to think about the cowboys and what she should do.

As she straightened her booth, the bell over the door rang and Sam stepped into the dim interior from the bright Texas sunlight.

Mona's pulse quickened, her heart leaping into her throat. She wasn't ready to face Sam or Grant. She hadn't had enough time to figure out what she wanted.

"Change into jeans," he said, without preamble. "We're going to the rodeo."

"Is that an invitation or a demand?"

"Whichever one works." He nodded toward the back. "Go on."

"I might have customers coming. It's not like I don't work during the day."

"Do you have customers this afternoon?"

"As a matter of fact, I don't. I had a run on rescheduling appointments." Her gaze narrowed. "Did you have anything to do with that?" She shook her head. "No. Of course not. How could you?"

He advanced toward her. "Are you going to change or am I gonna have to do it for you?"

Her body trembled at his threat. "Promises, promises."

Sam took another step.

Mona turned and ran, Sam following her up the steps to her apartment.

The last time she and Sam had been alone in her apartment for any length of time, they'd slept together. After Sam had made love with her and Grant, Mona wondered if he was still interested. She stripped the clothes she'd been wearing and moved about the apartment in her bra and underwear.

Sam stood at the door, his hat shading his eyes in the dim lighting of the room.

She gathered her jeans and a white blouse with a Vneckline she knew would display an ample amount of her cleavage. With the outfit in hand, she gave Sam one last chance, planting herself in front of him. "What? An almost naked woman stands in front of you and it doesn't even raise your blood pressure?"

"Oh, it's raised all right."

"Then why aren't you making a move?" She pressed her breasts against his chest. "Did our threesome change your mind about me?"

He grabbed her arms and set her away from him. "You're doing crazy things to me, and I want you enough to tear through your panties and fuck you until you can't walk anymore." He sighed. "But, Mona, I'm not the man for you."

Her pulse pounding through her veins at his coarse, sexy words, she blinked up at him. "You're not?"

"No. Relationships are hard enough when both people are totally committed to each other. I like you a lot, but I'm not sure I'm ready to commit." He brushed his thumb across her cheek. "In time, I know I'd grow to love you, but I just don't have that time and I won't ask you to wait for me."

She nodded. "Fair enough. At least you had the decency to tell me before it went any further." With the jeans and shirt still in her hand, she looked up at him. "No need to take me to the rodeo."

"Oh yes, there is. Get your clothes on, I'll be waiting in my truck." He pressed a kiss to her forehead. "You really are special and you deserve a man who loves you enough to sacrifice everything to win your heart."

"And that's not you." She leaned into him, inhaling

the scent of leather, denim and aftershave. A sense of loss washed over her along with a flood of relief. She really hadn't had enough time with Sam to fall in love with him and thankfully, she no longer had to choose between him and Grant. "Thank you, Sam. I hope we can stay friends."

"You bet." He slapped her ass. "Now get dressed. I want to find good seats." He left her apartment, his boots clunking down the steps.

Mona stood for a moment, the relief of a moment ago giving way to a tightening in her gut and constriction of her throat. Though she no longer had to decide between Sam and Grant or both, she still had to resolve within herself whether she trusted Grant enough to let him back into her heart.

When the thought hit her, she realized he'd never left her heart in the first place. All those years she hadn't dated, hadn't been interested in other men were because of Grant.

Mona threw her clothes on and jammed her feet into her cowboy boots. Grabbing her cowboy hat, she ran down the stairs and hopped up into Sam's truck. "Are we going to watch Grant ride?"

He nodded. "Uh huh." Shoving the shift into reverse, he backed out of the alley onto Main Street and turned the truck toward the rodeo arena.

Sitting forward, Mona couldn't wait to get there and see Grant. She'd come to a decision. Seeing him might help her solidify it.

Sam glanced over at her. "Did you know why Grant married Desiree?"

"He told me she was pregnant." She sat back, not wanting to think about Grant's ex-wife and that he'd gotten her pregnant.

"Did he tell you whose baby she was pregnant with?"

Her head whipped around. "I assumed it was Grant's."

Sam's lips thinned. "It was Dalton's."

"Then why did Grant marry her?"

"He didn't want her baby to suffer because of his and Dalton's actions. When Dalton refused to marry the girl, Grant stepped in to give the baby a father."

"What happened?" She'd heard through the rodeo grapevine that his wife had miscarried. "I can't imagine Grant divorcing her because she miscarried?"

"No, he's the type who'll stand by a woman even when there's no reason to stand by her anymore because he made a promise. He caught her in his bed with Dalton."

The man who'd refused to marry the woman pregnant with his child, took her to bed after she'd married Grant. Mona's stomach roiled. "The bastard."

"That's what ended his marriage and his partnership. He crawled into a bottle of whiskey and would have died there if I hadn't pulled him out of a ditch in North Dakota."

Mona leaned back against her seat, all her misconceptions about Grant swirling around her. He ditched her to do right by Dalton's pregnant mistress.

"Why are you telling me this?"

"I thought you should know. And Grant wouldn't

have shared unless you asked the right questions. He's not so proud of his alcoholic years."

Mona sat in silence the rest of the way to the arena.

The parking lot was full so Sam found a place to park in the grass and they walked to the arena.

Once inside, Sam found seats halfway up the stands overlooking the line of gates and chutes where a cowboy prepared to ride a bronc. He balanced on the railings of the bucking chute and eased down onto the sorrel horse, shifting and slamming against the rails. Then he gripped the rope and leather handle tied around a horse's belly, adjusting it to tighten his hold.

On the loudspeaker, the announcer called out the cowboy's name and the horse he was riding. While the crowd cheered, the cowboy laid back on the horse's hindquarters, gripping the strap between his legs, his heels at the animal's shoulders. When he gave a nod, the gate swung open.

The horse leaped from the chute, kicking out his hind legs, coming down hard on his front hooves, jolting the rider. His hat flew off, he lost his balance and was thrown over the animal's head.

The crowd rose to their feet with a synchronized gasp.

The man rolled to his feet and stood, and the audience roared their approval.

Mona's heart pounded and she gripped Sam's arm. "Doesn't that hurt?"

Sam nodded. "Sometimes more than others." He pulled a red bandana out of his pocket and waved it.

"Why are you doing that?"

"I made a promise. Now, listen."

The announcer's voice interrupted with, "Direct your attention to gate number six. Grant Raleigh, a native Texan, will be riding the toughest buckskin this side of the Brazos, Cowboy Killer."

Mona's fingers dug into Sam's arm. "He's going to ride a killer horse?" She half-stood. "I can't watch."

Sam pressed her back into her seat. "Sit and hush."

The voice on the loudspeaker went on. "Ladies and gentlemen, you are all in for a treat. Not only has Grant been a five-time All-Around Champion, he's been a four-time bareback champ, and an inductee to the ProRodeo Hall of Fame."

"He did all that?" Mona whispered.

Sam smiled. "Yes, ma'am."

Mona's pulse raced as Grant balanced on the railing, his gaze panning the crowd. When he saw Sam waving the red bandana, he nodded and settled onto the back of the buckskin.

The announcer continued, "I'm sorry to say this will be Grant Raleigh's last rodeo. He just announced today that he's retiring after this event to settle down and raise horses and cattle and maybe a family he hopes will be seen in future events."

The crowd booed, the boo turning into a chant, "We want Grant! We want Grant!"

Grant gripped the strap between his legs and pulled it tight. Then he laid back on the horse, his heels resting on the shoulders. At his nod, the gate swung open and the horse exploded out of the chute.

Mona stood, her heart in her throat as the beast's

front hooves slammed into the ground, then he twisted and turned, his back hooves kicking out, all four feet off the ground at once. Again and again, the horse bucked, kicked, hit the ground and started all over again.

Grant held on, his hat screwed down tight on his head, his left arm waving out to the side, his heels spurring the horse's front shoulders. A loud buzzer sounded over the roar of the crowd, and Grant sat up, both hands working to free himself from the strap. Two riders moved up beside the crazed horse, waiting for Grant to grab hold of one cowboy and slide to the ground.

Just as Grant freed his hand, the buckskin kicked the horse beside him, pivoted and launched himself in the other direction.

Grant flew into the air.

Mona slapped a hand to her mouth to smother her scream as Grant hit the ground hard on his back and lay motionless.

Cowboys rushed forward, the bucking horse was herded into a chute, and the crowd grew silent waiting for Grant to get up.

Sam shoved the red bandana into her hands and left her alone in the stands, racing down the steps. He hurdled himself over the fencing around the arena, landing in the soft dirt.

Mona didn't breathe as she pushed her way to the railing.

When she reached the metal barrier she waited, her heart missing beats, her hand pressed to her aching chest.

"Be okay. Please be okay," she whispered.

After a full two minutes had passed, Grant stirred. He reached up to Sam who took his hand and said something Mona couldn't hear.

Grant nodded and Sam pulled him slowly to his feet.

The people in the stands leaped to their feet, clapping and stomping their feet.

Tears streamed from Mona's eyes as relief washed over her.

"Folks, it's just like Grant to put on a show that will leave you on the edge of your seats," the announcer said. "Wait, I believe he'd like to say something to the crowd."

Grant waved a hand toward a man who brought out a wireless microphone, switched it on and handed it to him.

"Ladies and gentlemen. There's a special woman in the crowd I'd like you all to meet. Mona? Where are you?"

For a moment she didn't comprehend his words, then she raised the red bandana. She squealed as a couple of cowboys converged on her, lifted her up and over the railing. Two more cowboys reached up to catch her and set her on her feet in the dirt and led her to the center of the ring.

Grant stood before her, alive, a little battered, but beautiful to Mona.

"What are you doing?" she asked, afraid to breathe, terrified this was all a dream.

"Mona Daley, I haven't always been a good man, and you have every right to hate me, but you make me want to be better. I can't think of anyone else I'd rather spend my retirement with than you."

Sam leaned over and said, "On your knee, cowboy. Good grief, can't even get your dismount right." He shoved something into Grant's hand.

Grant dropped to his knee and took Mona's hand. "Mona, I'm done with the rodeo. I'm not going anywhere else in the world without you. I want to own a ranch and raise horses, cows and…a passel of kids that look just like you. Will you marry me?" He handed the mic to her and took her left hand, holding up a shiny diamond engagement ring.

Mona's eyes filled with tears and she spoke clearly into the mic, "Yes."

Grant slid the ring onto her ring finger, Mona handed the mic to Sam and she threw herself at Grant, knocking him over into the dirt.

He landed with an oomph. "Careful, I think one of my ribs is broken."

"And that, folks is how a cowboy leaves the rodeo!" the announcer said.

Mona eased off him, her face split in a grin she couldn't hide for a million dollars.

The crowd was on their feet cheering as Sam and Mona helped Grant out of the arena and to a waiting ambulance.

Medics checked Grant over while Sam stood with Mona.

"You knew about this?" she asked.

Sam's chest puffed out. "It was Grant's idea. I just helped it along."

"How did you get my appointments to cancel?"

"Bunny." Sam grinned. "She's got a devilish streak in her."

"Tell me about it." Mona turned to Sam. "And you're okay with this?"

"More than okay."

The tall, slender woman Mona had seen Grant leave the Ugly Stick Saloon with two nights before stepped up to Sam.

Mona's hackles rose.

"Hi, I'm Tacey. And you must be Mona, the woman who captured Grant's heart. Just to set the record straight, he refused to go to bed with me because he was still in love with you."

Grant limped across to them. "And believe me, she tried everything to seduce me."

Sam slid an arm around Tacey's waist and brought her forward. "I'm considering Tacey as my new ropin' partner."

Grant nodded. "You'll have your hands full if you take her on." He reached out for Mona. "And I'll have my hands full with the prettiest beautician in Texas."

Mona melted into his arms. Happier than she'd ever been in her life.

"When are you going to marry me?" Grant asked.

"How soon can we get a license? I'm afraid if I wait, you'll run off to another rodeo or something."

He shook his head. "The only rough riding I'm gonna be doin' is in bed with you."

Mona raised her hat and said, "Yee-haw!" Then she kissed her very own cowboy.

BOOTS & WISHES

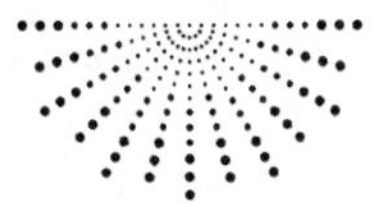

UGLY STICK SALOON SERIES BOOK #10

by
New York Times Bestselling Author
Elle James

writing as

Myla Jackson

BOOTS & WISHES
UGLY STICK SALOON
New York Times Bestselling Author
ELLE JAMES
writing as
MYLA JACKSON

CHAPTER ONE

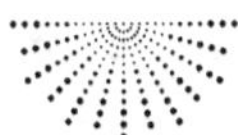

"Hey, cowboy, what say you strap on the chaps and we go for a ride?" Audrey stood in the doorway of the storeroom, wearing chaps over her blue jean cutoffs and carrying a leather whip coiled in one hand. In her other hand was a pair of man-sized leather chaps. They were the ones out of his closet from home. She liked him best in the real deal.

Jackson's eyes widened and he teetered, almost losing his balance on the ladder he had climbed up to change the bulb in the fluorescent light fixture hugging the ceiling. He held the long white tube he'd been about to install in the slot he'd just pulled the burned-out bulb from. "Now? Are you ovulating?"

"Do I have to be ovulating for you to want to make love to me?" Audrey's gut instantly knotted and her eyes stung. "Six months ago, you'd have dropped the bulb and leaped off the ladder at an offer like this." Her shoulders sagged and she sighed. "I was afraid of this."

Jackson set the new bulb in the slots and climbed down from the ladder. "Afraid of what?" He pulled her into his arms and kissed her forehead.

"Afraid making love would become a chore."

Jackson snorted. "Never."

"Admit it." She poked a finger at his chest. "Ever since we decided to try to get pregnant, we've lost some of the magic and spontaneity we used to enjoy."

When Jackson started to shake his head, Audrey raised her eyebrows and gave him a pointed look. "Be honest."

Jackson's head stopped in midshake and he grimaced. "Okay, so it's not quite as spontaneous as it used to be. But I love you and never get tired of making love with you."

"And I never tire of making love with you. But all the effort of timing our lovemaking is taking the joy out of our sex life." She stepped back and turned away from him, her heart sore. "Maybe we should give up trying. If it happens, it happens." She bit her bottom lip before continuing softly, "And if it doesn't, it wasn't meant to be. We weren't meant to be parents. I mean, my life has been anything but role-model material."

Warm, work-roughened hands curled around her arms and she was pulled back against Jackson's solid chest. "Sweetheart, it will happen. Most likely when we least expect it. And even if it doesn't—which I'm not giving up—you would be enough to keep me happy for the rest of my life. And you're the best role model a kid could have. You're real, tender-hearted, and you care about everyone you come in contact with."

Audrey's heart filled to overflowing. Jackson was the man who made her life complete. Her one true love. He loved her even with her background as a stripper. She couldn't imagine loving anyone else or living without him. She covered his hands on her arms and leaned back against him. "I love you, Jackson Gray Wolf. That will never change." Turning in his embrace, she cupped his cheek. His face was so dear to her and made her grateful every day of her life she'd found him. "I want to have your children. I want to see little Gray Wolf boys running around the ranch, learning to ride horses, swimming in the creek and raising hell like I'm certain you and your brothers did when you were growing up."

"And I want half a dozen little girls with strawberry-blond hair and eyes so blue they make the Texas skies pale in comparison."

"Nice." She slid her hands up his chest to lock behind his neck. "When did you become a romantic?"

"When I met you." He kissed her, his tongue sliding along the seam of her lips.

She parted her lips and teeth to him and his tongue, enjoying the way he stroked her, like having sex with their mouths. The man was everything a woman could want and more.

Tall, dark and handsome, with the high cheekbones and inky black eyes of his Kiowa ancestry. Dressed in jeans and a blue chambray shirt, he was a sexy mix of cowboy and Indian all wrapped up in a muscular package Audrey couldn't get enough of.

Her core tightened, her body warmed and she

backed away until her hand connected with the store-room door. With a quick twist, she locked the door.

Jackson's eyes flared and a smile tilted the corners of his lips. He reached for his belt buckle and flicked it open.

"Now you're getting the right idea," Audrey purred. She handed him the leather chaps and paused to cup the bulge growing behind his fly.

While Jackson tied the chaps around his hips, Audrey yanked her tank top up over her breasts and tossed it onto a case of whiskey. "I thought I'd have to dance a striptease for you to get you excited."

"Sweetheart, all you have to do is stand there and I'm as hard as a steel rod." He stalked her, his fingers making quick work of the buttons on his jeans, popping them free one at a time.

Audrey jerked her zipper open and slipped her shorts down her legs. Wearing nothing but her bra, red cowboy boots and chaps, her pussy creamed and she couldn't wait to mount her cowboy and ride him until they both came.

Her sexy husband scooped her up by the backs of her thighs.

She wrapped her legs around his waist and eased down over his rock-hard cock. "Mmmm. Now that's what I'm talking about."

Jackson backed her against the door and pinned her hands above her head in one of his big ones. "Soft and sweet, or make it rough?" he asked.

"Ride me, baby," she breathed, her pulse pounding, a

wash of juices easing his thickness inside her. "Make it hard and fast. I'm already teetering on the edge."

"I aim to please." He braced her against the wood door and drove into her deep, long and hard, pulled out and thrust into her again. In and out, he moved, his hips pumping, his cock thickening with every stroke.

He filled her so tightly she couldn't think of anything else but him and the way he made her feel.

The tension built, her body tightened around him, and her breasts beaded, her blood flowing hot through her veins as she climbed that exquisite path to release.

The tingling began at her core and spread outward as she climaxed. Then Audrey was riding the waves of her orgasm, her body shuddering deliciously.

Jackson thrust one last time, burying himself deep inside her. He released his hold on her wrists, gripped her hips in his big hands and held her, his body rigid, his member full and throbbing against the walls of her channel.

When he finally relaxed and bent to capture her lips with his, he whispered, "I'll never get tired of this."

"Me either."

A loud banging on the door made Audrey jump.

"Hey, we're about out of longnecks up front. Could you guys stop boinking long enough for us to serve the customers?" Charli Sutton, Audrey's assistant manager, knocked again. "I know you're in there."

"I'll be out in a minute," Audrey called out. "With the longnecks." Audrey sighed and gathered her clothing. "Sometimes I wish I'd never bought the Ugly Stick."

Before she could slip her shirt over her shoulders,

Jackson pulled her against him and tweaked a beaded nipple. "Then we might never have met. This place brought us together. In fact, if not for this place, you wouldn't have hired Libby. Who knows what manner of woman Mark and Luke would have ended up with?"

Audrey smiled. "They do love each other, don't they? I've never seen Libby happier. And her father is finally beginning to accept that Mark and Luke both are part of her life."

"You've done so much for everyone who has ever come through those doors, including me." Jackson smoothed the hair off her brow. "You know the most beautiful thing about you?"

"No, but I have a feeling you're going to tell me." Audrey's heart swelled at the love in Jackson's eyes.

"Sure, your breasts are luscious and ripe for the tasting. The swell of your hips makes me hard all over again. And your eyes are so blue...well, I could get lost in them."

"Go on," she encouraged, her cup overflowing with his love.

Jackson gathered her close and tipped her chin up, lowering his mouth to hover over hers. "It's your heart that makes you so beautiful. You have so much love, empathy and compassion for others that everyone you meet falls in love with you."

"But I only love you," she said, her breath mingling with his. "The woman-loves-a-man kind of lov—"

Jackson stole her words away with a kiss, and Audrey forgot what she was saying and gave in to the temptation that was Jackson.

When he allowed her up for air, she leaned her forehead against his chest. "Even if we never have a baby, I'll be content as long as I have you."

"Content?" Jackson chuckled. "That doesn't sound inspiring." He helped her slip her tank top over her head, pinching the tip of one nipple through the lace of her bra. "I hope you'll be more than content. Hmmm." He bent to hold her shorts for her, helping her slide them up her legs and button them, his rough fingers skimming the sensitive skin over her tummy. "I'll have to work on that. Next thing you know, you'll be sliding into comfortable and we'll be sitting in rocking chairs, trying to remember where we left our teeth."

Audrey laughed and buttoned his jeans for him. "I'd be perfectly happy to grow old with you, Jackson Gray Wolf. Rocking chairs on the porch of the ranch house sounds like heaven. We could watch our grandchildren running around in the yard, playing tag."

"And our children would be sipping tea on the porch with us. All grown up and beautiful like their mother."

"You mean handsome like their father," Audrey corrected.

Jackson paused, his brow puckering. "Hey, hasn't it been two weeks since you last ovulated?"

"Two weeks and three days."

He glanced down at her belly. "And?"

Audrey chewed on her bottom lip. "I'm three days late for my period."

A smile spread across Jackson's face. "Why didn't you tell me?"

She shrugged. "I didn't want to get our hopes up."

"Is it too soon to take a pregnancy test?" he asked, buckling his belt. "Want me to go get one from the drug store?"

"The drug store is closed, sweetie. It closed four hours ago." Audrey touched his arm. "But I have one in my purse."

"Take it," he demanded. "Go, pee on it or do whatever it takes. I can't believe you haven't done it already."

Again, Audrey chewed on her bottom lip, her heart beating irregularly, alternating between the happy staccato of excitement and the dull thud of anticipated disappointment. "What if it comes out negative?"

"You don't know until you try."

"I wanted so much to be pregnant by Christmas."

"We've only just started trying. You have to be patient."

"Just started? It's been six months!"

"Half a year. It's nothing."

"It's five pregnancy tests and five negative results." A lump formed in Audrey's throat and she swallowed hard before continuing, "I don't know if I can stand another disappointment with Christmas so close."

Jackson pulled her into his arms again. "Christmas will be great, with or without a baby in your belly."

"But I wanted so much to be carrying your child by then." Her eyes welled and she fought to hold back the tears. No matter how hard she tried, one slipped out and trailed down her cheek.

"Oh, baby." Jackson brushed away the tear. "Trust me. Everything will work out. I promise."

"How can you promise something you might not be able to deliver?"

"You are worrying far too much. It's probably messing up your reproductive system. Relax." He shook her shoulders like a coach at a ball game. "It'll happen."

"Okay." She laughed. "I'll relax. And I'll try to make our 'sessions' more spontaneous."

"Right now, we'd better get those longnecks out front before the natives get restless and break down the door." Jackson hefted a case of beer and headed for the door.

Audrey unlocked it, leaned up to kiss Jackson's cheek and then opened the door. "I love you, babe."

He winked. "I love you more."

Audrey grabbed a couple of bottles of whiskey and followed Jackson through to the bar, enjoying the way his jeans rode his narrow hips. Oh yeah, making love to this hunk of a human was easy. What was harder was getting pregnant. She prayed she hadn't waited too long to start trying. Was thirty-two too old to get pregnant? She knew women who kept having babies well into their forties.

After Jackson settled the case of beer on the floor behind the bar, he kissed Audrey again and rounded the bar to join his brothers and friends at a table.

"I'll be glad when you two finally get pregnant." Charli bent over the case of longnecks and pulled several bottles out, loading them into the trough filled with ice to chill.

"You and me both." Audrey bent to grab three more,

handing them to Charli. "I don't know what we're doing wrong. I should be five months along by now."

"You can't expect to get pregnant on your first attempt, hon. It's not that exact a science."

"Okay, I didn't expect it on our first attempt, but we're five months into this and…" She waved a hand. "Nothing."

Charli straightened. "Oh, sweetie, this is really eating at you, isn't it?"

Audrey nodded, once again fighting the ready tears. "I never thought I'd ever want children. Until I met Jackson. Now I can't imagine not having children. Can't you just see them? All dark-haired, dark-eyed little boys running barefoot and wild?"

Shaking her head, Charli hugged her. "I *can* imagine. And you'll make a great mother, Audrey. You're like a mother to all of us misfits. It's about time you had a dozen children of your own, instead of playing momma to all of us."

Audrey smiled at Charli. The pretty blonde had been with her almost as long as Audrey had owned the bar. She wasn't just an employee. She was Audrey's best friend and confidant. "I know I've been very self-absorbed lately. How's it going for you? Have you set a date yet? When are you two going to tie the knot, settle down and have children?"

"Hey, this conversation isn't about me and Connor. It's about you, your man and the family you're trying to have."

"You haven't set a date, have you?" Audrey crossed

her arms. "Do I need to have a talk with Connor? Is he the hold-out?"

Charli's face flushed red. "Don't talk to Connor. He's more than ready to get married. I'm the hold-out."

Audrey's arms fell to her sides. "What's wrong? Have you two had an argument?"

Her assistant manager avoided answering by helping Libby serve several customers who'd come to the bar for refills on their beer mugs. When Charli returned to the case of beer, Audrey was waiting.

Charli shrugged. "I don't know. I just want to be sure before I make as big a commitment as marriage."

"It's easy. If you love him."

"Maybe for you. I was ready to leave the Ugly Stick and Temptation to move to Austin before I met Connor. Now I'm not sure. I'm afraid I'll get restless again. I don't want to marry Connor, then get bored and leave. I would hate myself forever if I hurt him."

"That tells me you love him."

"Yeah, but is love enough?"

"Oh, honey, it is if you're willing to put your man's needs above your own, and he's willing to do the same."

Charli shrugged. "Well, I'm not good at the commitment thing."

"You've been living with him going on almost a year. I'd say you're pretty well committed."

"Sort of, but marriage is so much more." Charli settled more bottles in the trough and straightened. "I'm not sure I'm ready."

"Can you imagine living without him?"

Charli's eyes widened. "Hell no."

"Then there you have it."

Charli smiled. "You make it sound easy."

Audrey shook her head. "Nothing's easy about relationships, whether you're married or living together. It helps when you're muddling through it all if you love each other. And I've seen you two together. There's love in spades."

"Thanks, Audrey. Once again, you're all full of advice for everyone else. You need to take some for yourself." Charli hugged her. "Relax. It will happen when it happens."

"Gah!" Audrey threw her hands in the air. "If I hear one more person say that, I'm liable to throw something. We've been married long enough I think it'll stick. But I'm in my thirties and not getting any younger."

"Please don't say you're getting old. You look like you're nineteen."

"But I'm not nineteen, Charli. I can hear my biological clock ticking so loudly I can't hear myself think. At one time in my life I thought owning my own business and having friends would be enough."

"You've accomplished more than most people have in their fifties."

"Sure. I have the Ugly Stick Saloon." She'd been so happy when she'd bought the bar, using her hard-earned stripping money. "I have the best employees I can trust and count as my friends."

"Darn right you do. And we'd do anything for you. You've bailed more than one of us out of tight spots."

"I thought this place was all I needed." Audrey stared

out across the saloon, packed with patrons. Friday night was always crowded. Her gaze gravitated toward the man she loved. "Until I met Jackson, I thought I had it all. Now I want more."

"And by more, you mean a family to call your own?"

Audrey nodded. "My life won't be complete until I have Jackson's children."

"You have our prayers and wishes. And you can count on me to babysit." Charli frowned. "Damn. You're making me rethink my position on marriage. All of the sudden, I've been bitten by the baby bug."

Audrey's heart lightened and she grabbed Charli's hands. "Wouldn't it be great if we were both pregnant at the same time? Our kids could grow up together."

"Whoa! Wait a minute. One step at a time." Charli pulled her hands free. "I promised my momma I'd wait to have children until I was properly married. I don't plan on breaking my promise to my mother, God rest her soul. Let's work on you first. You can pave the way and show me how easy it is before I commit to marriage, babies and the whole nine yards."

Audrey nodded. "Okay then. Let's see if my trucks are loaded with asphalt."

Charli's brows furrowed. "Huh?"

"I'm a few days late for my period. I hope to be paving soon." She squared her shoulders and reached beneath the bar for her purse and the pregnancy kit she'd tucked inside a week ago. Either way, she wanted to know whether or not she was pregnant.

"Oh, Audrey, that's great. I have my fingers crossed for you and Jackson." Charli held up both hands, displaying four sets of crossed fingers. "I'd cross my toes if I wasn't wearing these darned boots." She gave Audrey a nudge. "Go, pee on the stick or whatever it is you do with one of those. Do you want me to go with you?"

"No. I can manage on my own. I've been peeing by myself for thirty-two years." With excitement building, Audrey tried to catch Jackson's eye as she walked toward the hallway where the bathrooms were. He was deep in conversation with Mark and Luke. Probably about ranch business.

Oh well. She'd come out in a few minutes with their happy news. She had to believe the sixth time was a charm. It was going to happen.

Audrey entered the bathroom and tore open the box, her hands suddenly shaking, all her hopes for the future wrapped up in that one little box and the magic stick inside.

All she needed was to pee on the test strip, plug it into the stick and wait for the results. She'd even sprung for the more expensive test kit—the one that spelled it out. Either it would say *Pregnant* or *Not Pregnant*. No interpretation required.

When she hovered over the toilet, her knees shook and she struggled to let loose a stream of urine. The last couple of times, she'd had trouble with this, as if not peeing on the strip would change the results.

Drawing on Jackson and Charli's advice, she relaxed and eventually peed. Shoving the test stick beneath the warm urine, she almost dropped it, she was trembling so badly. Five seconds was all she needed. Thankfully, when she pulled it out, it was damp at the right end of the device.

As she waited the required three minutes, her breath lodged in her throat. Audrey checked her watch. One minute down, nothing on the display screen. She closed her eyes and counted to one hundred, opened her eyes and checked her watch. Two minutes down. A quick glance at the stick's display window and it was empty.

She took a ragged breath, her heart thundering, her eyes burning. Sitting on the toilet for the last minute was sheer torture. Closing her eyes, she prayed harder than she'd ever prayed before. *Please, God, give me a baby.*

Avoiding the test stick, she checked her watch. Four minutes had passed. Turning her gaze to the window, the first word she saw was *Pregnant.*

Her heart leaped into her throat before she saw the other word beside it.

As quickly as her hopes had skyrocketed, they crashed to the earth.

There in the display window were the two words she'd dreaded.

Not Pregnant.

ABOUT THE AUTHOR

Twenty years of livin' and lovin' on a South Texas ranch raising horses, cattle, goats, ostriches and emus left an indelible impression on Myla Jackson, one she likes to instill in her red-hot stories. Myla pens wildly sexy, fun adventures of all genres including historical westerns, medieval tales, romantic suspense, contemporary romance and paranormal beasties of all shapes and sexy sizes. or spending time with her family. She lives in the tree-covered hills of Northwest Arkansas with her husband of more than 20 years and her muses—the human-wanna-be canines—Chewy and Sweetpea.

To learn more about Myla Jackson and her alter ego Elle James visit:
www.mylajackson.com
mylajackson@mylajackson.com

ALSO BY MYLA JACKSON

Ugly Stick Saloon Series

Boots & Chaps (#1)

Boots & Sex Ed (#2)

Boots & Leather (#3)

Boots & Promises (#4)

Boots & Bareback (#5)

Boots & Dirty Tricks (#6)

Boots & Lace (#7)

Boots & Roses (#8)

Boots & Buckles (#9)

Boots & the Wishes (#10)

Boots & Twisters (#11)

Boots & the Bachelor (#12)

Boots & The Rogue (#13)

Boots & The Heartbreaker (#14)

Boots & Wings (#15)

Tomb Raider Trouble

Trouble with Harry

Trouble with Will

Trouble with Mitch

Bound and Tied

Honor Bound

Duty Bound

River Bound

Paranormal

Shewolf

Thorn's Kiss

Sex, Lies & Vampire Hunters

www.ingramcontent.com/pod-product-compliance
Lightning Source LLC
Chambersburg PA
CBHW070948120726
47910CB00004B/1160